THE TALL OWL

AND OTHER STORIES

COLUM SANSON-REGAN

THE TALL OWL AND OTHER STORIES
© 2020 Colum Sanson-Regan
Front cover © David Norrington, owl illustration © Adobe
Stock.

British Library Cataloguing in Publication Data.
A catalogue record for this book is available from the
British Library.

Published in the United Kingdom by
Wordcatcher Publishing.
www.wordcatcher.com
Facebook.com/WordcatcherPublishing

First Edition: 2020
Paperback format ISBN: 9781789422948
Ebook format ISBN: 9781789423617
Category: Short Story Collection

CONTENTS

BORN IN A FIRE

I was born in a fire. On the morning I was born, Mama walked the misty river to the café to start the preparation in the kitchen. At Millers Cross, the forests are steep on both sides where the river rolls down and the two roads meet, forced together by the mountains, like the travellers that stop there. In the mornings the fog fills the valley like an artery. Mama worked in the café there at Millers Cross. It had just a few tables inside, and a kitchen. Most of the seats were at the back, outside near the river. Before she started, no one in the valley had ever tasted empanadas. Now everybody loved them. The café was always busy. The travellers stopped, drank coffee, ate her empanadas and sat in the garden. They stretched their legs along the path and looked at the silent, thick trees and the passing water. If you sat long enough, you'd see animals appear from the undergrowth on the other side. Deer, wild cats, otters, river rats. But most people didn't. They got back in their cars and drove away, moving onto the long roads, winding out of sight. This was Mama's place of peace. Even when the car park was full and the queues were slow, the smell of freshly baked cakes, breads and stuffed sweet empanadas meant everyone was nice to everyone else. For months she was nodded to and greeted on the street and in the café by the locals. 'Not long now' or, 'It'll be a boy you know', they said loudly from the counter, and if she served the dishes they'd send her good wishes all the way back to the kitchen.

Mama walked every morning from the hunting lodge about a mile upriver where she rented a room. Mister Emmets had taken her in. He was a lawyer who worked in the city. He owned the lodge and the café too, and he was the one who gave her the job. When he was in the café, he always sitting at a large plate and smiling at a full glass. He called out hello and waved at anyone who came in. On the weekend he sat in the back, thanking Mama each time she brought him a fresh coffee or beer. He was the only one who stayed long enough to see the animals appear on the other side of the bank. He had that thing that some people have. Knowing where to look at just the right time. And the animals didn't run when he saw them like they did with everyone else. He just had a way of being still. Sometimes he came in just in time for closing, with his hunting hat and his rifle over his shoulder. It didn't take long for him to trust Mama with opening and closing the café. She was seventeen years old then, a thin silhouette in the morning river mist, walking the mile to the café. But I was growing in her. Over the months this silhouette distorted, filled like a pouch.

Mama says she was heavy with me that morning. In the kitchen the worktops were covered with the ingredients and utensils: the powder, the soda, yeasts, all the fruits, creams, knives, whisks, all laid out in the order she'd need them. She had just turned the gas when she heard a giant's growl outside. That's what she said about the noise. The growl of a giant. She turned and looked through the kitchen delivery hatch and outside the front window she saw the eyes of a dragon, swooping down through the fog. The growl reached inside her, grabbing me and shaking me. She felt me jerk and jump. Then the huge flat passionless face of a truck appeared and before she had time to bless herself, it burst through the door and wall. It broke and crushed and scattered the furniture and it pushed through the wall of the kitchen. Then she was on the floor in falling bricks and steam. The truck didn't stop, it hit the ovens and the dragon's breath flashed, and everything burned. For a second, the air screamed, turned white, and then, as it rolled by it pulled the flame and the heat followed the rush as the truck smashed through the back of the café.

There was a moment. Mama was on the floor, on her back. The noise and heat were gone. In the back garden the truck slowed and stopped. We're alive, she thought. And then she saw the ceiling above her come down. It smashed onto the counter and broke around her. There was dust and darkness and a searing noise in her head. A wave of burning and the fizzing and popping of the hot dust-filled air washed over her, and then the giant's hand grabbed inside her body and squeezed. Her heart jumped wildly as her body convulsed, then my body moved, and the push started. I was coming.

This is how I was born. In the fire. Everyone in the valley was woken by the noise of the crash. They knew she was in there, making the empanadas with me inside her. Neighbours jumped out of bed and rushed. Figures appeared out of the fog, like crossing from one world to another. Albert was running with soaking blankets shouting, 'Get more, get more, she's in here', while Molly crouched at the gap of the tiny concrete tent, calling into the darkness, saying,' 'My God, the baby, it's coming, just push, I'm here.' The heat was growing and as much as Albert and now Donny from the mechanics across the road could do they couldn't stop the flames from spreading. Then the smoke started. The air was running out and Mama's body tightened. Molly was shouting louder and calling Donny and Albert, and the spasms grew more and more intense and my mother's body pushed me out. There were explosions of cannisters in the cabinets. More shouts now, more neighbours appearing with blankets dipped in the river and buckets and baskets of water, and then there were the noises of the voices and the burning, the snap of wood falling, the air crackling and fizzing full with kitchen debris, spores and chemicals. Then Donny was next to Molly with a wire cutter. He cut through the bloody chord with the garage tool. There was an explosion, another burst of chemical flame and debris. Molly took me in her arms and ran. Donny and Albert tried to drag my mother by her legs out of the concrete and wood tent, but when they moved her, she screamed a scream that cut through the air and everyone there. So, Donny tried to get closer. He cleared the rubble from around her. Her face was covered by a broken piece of scaffold. Albert moved around the other side and tried to shift the piece of wood, but she screamed again, so they covered her and the debris in a damp blanket and carried her to the riverbank. Mister Emmets arrived then. It had taken him less than eight minutes to run the mile with his rifle on his back and he crouched by my mother as they laid her down. She held his hand. 'You're OK,' he said. 'You have your baby. Girl. It's a girl. It's a girl.' She passed out then. It was still before 8:00 am. The neighbours had stopped the fire with the river water. The café was a smouldering heap in the valley thick with fog and smoke. The piece of scaffold fixed to Mama's head was held in place by a large iron nail. The

4

nail was embedded in the front of Mama's skull. They cut the scaffold away. They left the nail. I was washed in river water. My skin was marked in white and yellow spots and patches. They say I didn't stop crying for two days. When I did, it was when Molly sang 'Sally Moves Through the Rushes' over and over. So, Mama called me Sally. The markings didn't fade.

The nail was never removed from Mama's head. It stuck into her brain, and the doctors thought removing it was more dangerous than leaving it in. After the accident a fierce woman emerged. She stopped baking. She found arguments. Her tempers became a conversation currency in the valley, but everyone loved her because she, and I, were miracles. She lived with her miracle, sticking out of her head like a grotesque horn. She cleaned it, waxed it. She rubbed it when lost in thought. You get used to it, she said.

She's Mama Unicorn, Uni, and I'm Sala, like a salamander.

* * *

Mister Emmets' big smile disappeared. While the travellers' cars passed the site of the destruction and the locals worried about when he would rebuild the café, he was only working on one thing. From the day of the crash, when he'd watched the ambulance drive away from the riverbank, he'd vowed to hold the trucking company to account. He spent weekends at his office in the city. That company had government owners and everything that could be put in his way was, but he was determined. He stayed late in the city every night and when he came back to the lodge, he'd make sure there was enough money for Mama to take care of me before he left early the next morning. She wasn't able to work in the town. No one wanted to work with her anyway, and she certainly didn't want to work with them.

By the time he got the case to be seen, I was a speckled little girl, walking around the hunting lodge, pushing open the thick doors, holding consultations and negotiations with the dead animals' heads on the walls. There were lots of places to hide in the lodge and I'd hide from Mama for as long as I could when she shouted and stormed. And she did. She did for three years until one night, Mister Emmets came back and he had won. His smile returned. The settlement was enough for Mama to never have to worry about money again he said. Enough to rebuild a new café, make it a diner even. She would own it and run it. All of the money she made from her empanadas would be profit. She asked for the money up front, then announced she would move into the city to attend university. That was that. So at the age of four, I was attending university with my mother.

* * *

She studied anatomy then biological science. She took me with her, into the classrooms and lecture halls. Nobody stopped her. Mama was a lot calmer now she had a focus, but she was still impossible to argue with. Even if you were prepared, there was an intensity she had that could strike you. You think you're in control and then you're a bowling pin. There was no choice but to let whatever she wanted to happen, happen. I'd stand by her side and accept the embarrassed looks and glances of pity from whoever she was shouting at. She wore a shawl to cover her nail, but she couldn't hide me. Everybody wants to see the little girl to say how pretty she is, they just don't expect the little girl to have the skin of an amphibian. The other students and lecturers

6

accepted me, they brought me colouring and puzzle books to help me through the classes. Mama called me 'my special Sal'. She told me about the human body and all about my skin. My dermographism. That was the word I used when people asked. Usually they didn't. Mister Emmets called to the flat sometimes. He'd drop in and make sure that Mama was alright, and bring me animal picture books and I'd colour them in.

When I asked about my father she said, that's just what animals do. He disappeared up into the mountains, he ran off. She didn't blame him. She was scared too. They were young when it happened and when you're young you get scared. He was from a town further up the valley. He'd come to help with the fish nets when the spawning season started and this one time he stayed for the summer. He didn't have any education except fish. He had beautiful blue eyes and a way of looking into the distance which made Mama sure he was thinking of nothing at all. He never talked about any dreams, she said. When she told him she thought she was pregnant he left to go back upstream and she never saw him again. Her parents threw her out. Mister Emmets took her in.

* * *

Mama got a job in the university research laboratories. I started attending a school. I knew I looked weird. The white and yellow blotches on my face varied in size, and my thin lips glowed red. But still, within a few terms, I began to wear my baseball hat backwards. The years progressed. Within the class, friendships flowed and snapped, changed and turned around, but I saw that as with mine so did everyone else's. As I grew with the class, I started to forget about my face. Even my hands stopped taking my attention when I was writing. The class and

7

the teachers were used to my bizarre appearance. The strange was familiar, and after all, I laughed like them, I learned like them.

But as I grew older, into my teens, it changed. Dressed, I was fine, but what about when I, or someone else, a boy maybe, would want to take my clothes off? My breasts were growing and my body was thinning, but my skin was so discoloured, in some places it looked cracked like an overheated vase and in others blotched like a shallow scummy pond. No boy would want to see me undressed. Every time I thought of this, I collapsed into myself again. I disgusted myself. I was changing but my skin wasn't. A real salamander would shed its skin. I was trapped in a shell from the dirty riverbed. When Mama came back from the lab to the apartment in the evenings and took her shawl off, I found myself gazing at the nail. It was noisy there in the city, and she would read with such concentration, rubbing her nail and I would feel the animal patterns on my skin even more. When she was with me, I was always aware of how different, how strange, we were. When we were together I couldn't forget. And I started to hate that bit of metal.

* * *

Every year in the city there was a great fire, lit for one night at the beginning of the winter months. The city centre stopped, and people brought things they wanted to be rid of: old boxes, furniture, clothes, talismanic symbols and dolls. There was always something ready to be burned. There is magic in fire, the hypnotic power of the flame. People were drawn to it. People wanted to feed it. Couples and families fed the fire with the tattered edges of their lives, and didn't want to leave, didn't want the fire to die. I started to go by myself and would sit with

8

my hood up, staying there for as long as possible, getting as close as I could to that burning heart. One year I came home late and Mama said that she could afford to have me fixed. No more lizard skin she said. There was a doctor who'd agreed to try to change my skin. They would start somewhere on my body, not my face first, but there is a way. she said. At last she could make me better. She thought it would fill me with joy and hope. It didn't. It terrified me.

So I ran. It's what animals do. I went to the mountains. I was fifteen years old. The train went through the forests and came out on the other side, above the tree line, with peaks and lakes and clear skies. The river here was thin and fast, and I looked for work. People had to look twice at me, or three times. At the start I asked in shops and bars for work, but was too young, everyone asked me how I came to be up here all alone and what was wrong with my face. I ended up in the kitchen of a café. It was run by Angela. Angela didn't ask me any questions.

* * *

Mister Emmets tracked me down. I recognised his voice. It was light and friendly as he chose his dinner. His order came through. As I prepared it, I heard him talk with Angela.

'Have you seen a girl with a speckled face?'

Angela didn't answer straight away. There was a pause. I stood completely still and held my breath.

'A speckled face? What do you mean?'

'Marks on her face, white patches. She left home, she's young. I'm a friend of her mother.'

'I'm sorry, I haven't seen anyone like that.'

'OK, well listen, I'm staying here tonight, just across

9

the road, if you think of anything just ask for Emmets. We just need to know if she's alright. Her mother is very worried. She ran away, you know?'

* * *

At the end of the shift I left the café and he was waiting.

'So you knew I was there?'

'Here, let me walk you.'

But we didn't walk home. We walked further up the mountain. He told me about Mama, how worried she was, but then, I knew she would be. I could see her lying awake in the small apartment, listening to the noise of the night city outside, talking aloud to me, to the empty space where I should be, getting up and putting oil on her horn and turning on the lamp, opening another book.

'This is where I need to be. Maybe not here exactly, but somewhere that's not with her.'

It sounded awful saying it out loud like that.

'You know what it's like. You can't reason or talk with her. She just wants to tell me what to do. Who knows, maybe I'll meet my father up here.'

'Maybe you will. Your Mama has worked so hard to make it possible for you to do something about yourself. These doctors can change you, make you better, so that you can go through life without this… stigma. It can be easier.'

'What if I don't want that? I was born in a fire.'

He stopped walking then. So did I. It's so quiet in the mountains at night.

'Then what will you do?'

'Maybe go higher. Go higher into the mountains. You know what? Maybe I've already met my father. Maybe I made him a meal, or he gives me my change in the supermarket. There's no way of knowing.' I started walking again.

He stayed where he was. His voice followed me up the path, and that emotion, that pleading, was what I was climbing away from. I wanted the hills to be quiet again. 'Sala, I must tell Uni I know where you are. That you're safe. Your Mama, she's the bravest woman. All she wants to do is protect you and give you the best chance you can have. Her studies, her work, that's all for you. You can't hide from the world. Do what you want, but the world will find you. She wants to make sure no one can take advantage of you, do you see? Come back to the city with me. Or come to Millers Cross. Just to where I know you will be safe.'

Over my shoulder I said, 'You don't know where I will be safe. Was Mama safe in Millers Cross?'

That stopped him talking for a while. He walked after me. I waited. By now it was a smooth, clear, bright night. It was getting cold. He stopped just on the slope before me, so he was looking up at me. We stood like that for a while, looking at each other.

'You don't have your rifle.'

He smiled a broad smile. 'It's so good to see you Sal. It's so good. Tell me, how much did Uni tell you about your father?'

I pulled my collar up against the thin mountain air and he did the same, and I told him all about the fishing boy who ran away scared as we walked in step along the dark rocky path that wound up the mountain. I told him what my mother told me about him, about how he gave her the job and a place to live, how he sat in the garden and spotted the animals on the riverbank, I told him what she told me about the fire, about that morning, about the truck and the giant's voice, and the fire and

11

Albert and Donny and Molly. By the time I finished we were on the ridge. The sky was open wide and the valley was deep, colours of the mountain night spread wide before us, above and below, all blues and charcoal, olive dark and thick boot blacks, and we looked to the relief of the sharp peaks echoing into the distance.

He said, 'Even when it's dark it's beautiful up here. I can see why you'd stay.'

* * *

And I did. Angela kept me working. There was a spot on the river where the ground flattened and the water pooled. It was a steep walk up from the café. There was an old boat. I cleaned it and tied it to the bank. I started to work on it, to build a cover and make it warm. Everything I had fitted in the boat. It was so quiet. In the mornings in the half-light the deer would come and drink. There was one young deer which came by itself. Its markings looked like a leaf pattern drawn by a child. This high, the soil was weak, and stones poked through like knuckles and knees. I started to want to be on the edge of things. I climbed the rocks to the ridges. I saw how the thin river here found its way, slipping through the gaps. There were places where I could see the roads disappearing into the trees and fog thick in the valley below. Cars, trucks, vans, bikes, people, were all swallowed. From up there it's easy to believe in giants and dragons.

Emmets came hunting and each time he did, he would call in on me. He stopped asking me to come back. He'd joke that I should go hunting with him; I had natural camouflage. I showed him where I lived.

Emmets said, 'This isn't normal. Do you think this is normal? For a sixteen-year-old girl to be living on a boat in the mountains?' Then he got back in his car and he too was swallowed. The fourth time I saw him, I had a letter prepared. He promised to show it to her. He told me that she wasn't getting any better; that sleep had all but left her completely.

The letter was short. It just said, 'Darling Mama. Take care of yourself, I will take care of myself. I just want to live, maybe even to love. Thank you for everything you have done Mama. I will contact you when I am ready.' She'd spent enough of her life worried about me now, trying to make it all better for me, looking for ways, looking for more and more in books, squinting through the microscope. I wasn't a puzzle. I didn't want a solution. Right now, I just wanted to sit up above the tree line. Up where the ground is exposed and you can see the cold brutality of the rock we all build on. Where you sit on the edge and the land is crooked and scarred and huge. The mountains are castle walls, and the little towns are sentry points, lookouts for the teeming busy distracted humanity below. The air on the mountain is thinner than the city, it's colder and moves faster. Up here, you can see the weather coming. You can see it, but you can't stop it. You can't stop a storm. You can't stop an avalanche. You can only shout, 'Look out, look out!'

* * *

When I was ready, I went back to the city. But when I got there, she was gone.

I knocked on the neighbour's door and they told me she said she was going back to take care of her mother. She never spoke about her mother. I went to Millers Cross.

This was the only time I had been here since I was

three years old. The café was there, at the end of the steep valley road. It was a diner now. Today there were lines of motorbikes parked outside. Inside, there was a framed picture of my mother from a newspaper on the wall, the nail protruding from her head, holding me. I was a baby, my eyes were closed, my skin blotchy. She was so young, just a teenager, but her eyes were solid like compressed rock. She was looking straight at the camera, someone who should have been dead but instead, the truth of the world had been forced into her and now she had to live with it. She was holding me up as if to say, 'See? This is the truth'. The headline was 'Survivors'.

I remembered what my mother had said about the mechanic who cut me from her in the burning building, so I crossed the road. The garage was old. There was a shadow leaning over a car.

'Hello,' I called. The shadow straightened up. He was in his sixties, but he could have been ancient, the way he came out to the light. He stopped in his approach and then stuttered, 'Sala, is that you? Really? All grown up. You're so beautiful. You've come back. Sala? So beautiful. How is Uni, your Mama?'

When I told him why I was there he said, 'No, she never came back. When you see her, tell her that we still think of her. I miss her. Nobody bakes empanadas anymore.'

I thanked him and crossed the road back to the diner. I ordered a coffee and looked out the back window. It was getting late. The darkness was coming down the river.

Emmets came in. He had his rifle. When he saw me, he hugged me, held me for longer than he had before. His jacket smelt damp and old. He must be old now too,

I thought, before he let go.

'It's good you're here, so good. She's here you know. Why don't you stay? You said in your letter that you wanted to love. "Maybe even to love," you said, but love is more than between just a guy and a girl.'

'You read my letter?'

'Sala, there's love for family too you know. Don't discount that one. It's stronger really. Your mother was so quiet before the accident, a different person. Now, you know, she's... she's a better woman, she's always been a better woman with you. I know, she shouts and gets angry, in a way she's crazy, but she's a better woman. But since you left she's more... difficult. She hates her horn. She's been to doctors again trying to find a way, to take it out. They won't help her, just give her drugs for her moods. She'll love to see you.' He looked at me keenly as he drank his coffee. 'You're stronger too, I can see it.'

When we walked out, he told me to go to the lodge. He had a deer on the back of the truck. A young deer, with leaf markings and a single bullet wound in its neck. Blood dripped onto the truck. It upset me all of a sudden. It made me shudder.

'How could you kill her like that? How could you do it?'

'Sala, come on. You know I hunt. My rifle, what did you think it did?'

'How can you have that part to you Emmets, when you seem like such a caring man?'

'I am a caring man Sala. A caring man with a rifle.'

'Will you come with me now?'

'I'll come later Sala. You two need to be together.'

* * *

15

The lodge was easy to find. The path from the café was well worn. I didn't remember it from the outside. Its size surprised me. It loomed over the riverbank. And as soon as I stepped inside, I remembered it all, the wooden floors, the antlers for coat hangers, the thick beams, the slow doors. In my memory it was always a bright afternoon, the sun reflecting off the floors, but it was getting dark now. I went into the main room. A fire slumbered in the hearth. The animal heads were still on the walls: deer, wolf, otter, elk. They looked shabbier than I remembered. They all looked down on the long table. Sitting there was Mama. The nail in her head caught the erratic colour pulse of the flames, and she looked like a beautiful ghoul, a spirit of a violent end haunting the lodge. In front of her, laid out on the thick table, was a selection of surgeons' and machinists' tools, a bundle of swabs and bandages, a bell of clear liquid and a tub of thick wax. She had a surgeon's knife in her hand when she looked up at me. Then she saw me, and her weeping rolled from her and across the room, and when she spoke there was a heaviness in her voice which was never there before, the words could barely rise above the sobbing. 'Sally! Now? Sally, now you come back?'

I went and crouched next to her, holding her. 'Mama, I'm sorry for staying away. I'm back, I'm back.' As I held her and she sobbed, I looked at the array of tools she had put in front of her. 'Mama, all this…'

Then she straightened up and pushed me back. Keeping her eyes on mine, with that intensity, that force, and her teeth clenched, she picked up a clamp and put it to the end of the nail.

'Mama. Mama. You don't want this.'

'No Sally, you don't want this. We're not the same.

16

I wasn't born like this.' Her words were so heavy and slow, 'I remember what it's like. I do, Sally, I do. I'm so tired of being, being this me, with this thing in my head. This angry voice. This piece of giant. I don't want to shout anymore. Sally, you don't want to be fixed. I do. I need to take it out.' Her voice was dragging itself around and around the room, back to the same point each time. Help me. She'd keep circling until what she wanted to happen happened. Help me. I looked at her head, at the nail, at this freak, this angry wonder of survival. She'd already cut away at her scalp around the nail and applied the wax. It was oily and red, glistening like a scarred fish. I could smell the surgical spirits from the jar. The fire burned low, glowering at the end of the room. The walls leaned in. The heads on them were old, their hides were mottled and their eyes were clouded. This place could fall apart in an instant. A big fire would finish it. It could all be over in a few burning moments. I took the clamp. Just before I spoke, a smell of empanadas passed me, just for a second and then was gone.

'Do I just pull?'

'Yes, Sally, just pull.'

'Tell me what to do Mama.'

'Tighten it on the horn. Yes, like that. Tight? OK, here are the ring forceps. This one, yes. To hold the scalp down. Push down. Secure? Now pull Sally. Slowly. Pull.'

WHAT YOU CAME
HERE FOR

Marley was growing out from the waist. He was big to start with anyway, but ever since they'd got off the plane, that ring around his middle kept expanding and expanding. Everyone here was so small and slim, he felt like he was taking up too much room, and he lumbered around like a guilty giant. Brady set up the locked off shot and adjusted the aperture. The extra light pushed some shadows back, but Marley's unhappy bulk blocked so much out. His face was heavier too. Over the weeks, his smile had been pushed down under the weight of that face. His chin was disappearing, and by the time the deadline for the filming was put back for the for third time, no expression had a chance, each one just slid right off, leaving a drag of disgust. Marley had to stop pretending he could do anything about it. It was all down to Soraya.

Soraya. The one in control of when the filming could start. Though, no surprise, Brady and Marley had never spoken to her. For the last three weeks, everything had come through Sam Ju, and as the messages and reasons why not pulled hard on the thread, Marley was spending more of his time in big bodied anger, pulling out profanities then cursing his empty pockets. He threatened to leave and go home, but Brady knew he wouldn't. The only thing that was greater than Marley's anger was his devotion to the promise of money. Being this close to Soraya's wealth made him sweat and Brady could sense how he wanted to rub up against it.

Brady refocused. Marley moved out of the frame and paced up and down the studio pushing his phone to his slippery face.

'I know I haven't paid for it yet,' he shouted. 'We've been through this, you have my deposit, I've told you it'll come through, Jesus, it's not like I can go anywhere anyway.'

Brady moved to the other side of the studio to set up the lights. As he loosened one, it turned and shone directly on to Marley who put up his hand in front of his face and squinted.

'I've had it with this shit storm Brady, this is it. I'm sick of this bastard country.'

Marley waved through the glass to the control room.

'Ping! Ping, get in here.'

Ping came through the door nodding and looked up at him. She only came up to the top of his belly.

'Delay?'

'Ping, can you tell that little jizz monkey who's on sound that we need to reset?'

'Ping,' said Brady from the dark corner, 'can you sit in the chair for a moment please? For a light test?'

Ping smiled at Brady and sat. Marley swatted the air with his big hands and stared through the glass at the sound controller. Brady looked through the viewfinder before turning another lamp, setting the angle.

'Think she's about the same size?'

'They're all the same size,' Marley stood in front of

Ping and pointed to the control room. 'Reset sound! Re – Set.'

Ping went back to the control room and closed the door. Through the glass, Marley and Brady watched her and the sound controller talking back and forth, both of them glancing into the studio. Marley said, 'Do you ever get the feeling she's not translating what I've asked her to? That the two of them just talk about what an asshole I am?'

'They do seem to have a lot to say.' Brady adjusted the glow.

Fifteen minutes later Soraya walked through the door.

* * *

When someone so utterly beautiful enters a room, things change. Every ion, every molecule, alters its orientation to pay attention. Her eyes were gemstones moving though the room, her hair was tied up in two tight buns, her slim shoulders carried poise and strength and when she stopped and stood in the centre of the studio, the light behind her made a shimmering halo. Marley straightened his back and wiped his hand across his middle.

'So wonderful to meet you, finally,' was what he said. 'Thank you so much for coming and doing this. We can't wait, it's going to be great.'

Soraya had two Chinese men with her, one of whom extended his hand.

'Hello I'm Sam Ju. Soraya has got one hour today that is all.'

'One. One hour. Let's get moving then.'

Brady put the small circular table patterned with a glass mosaic of a yin and yang symbol next to the seat.

Soraya sat down. Ping came in with a face brush which she fluttered around Soraya's face.

Brady said, 'Is this light OK?'

'Aren't you going to say how nice it is to meet me?'

That stopped him for a moment, but then he said, 'It's lovely to meet you. Is this light OK? Not too bright?' He picked the lapel microphone up and knelt beside her, fixing it to her dress.

'Can I get a beer?'

'Shouldn't you say nice to meet you too?'

She smiled at that. He stood up and Marley was right in front of him, with his hand on his hips, taking up all the space.

'She wants a beer,' he said and sidestepped Marley.

'Brady, just set will you? Ping! Ping! A beer? What kind of beer Soraya? Mr Sam Ju, what kind of beer would she like? We can send someone out…'

He checked the frame and it was centred on Marley's belly and crotch. Soraya peeked around and smiled into the camera. 'Of course. Nice to meet you. Brady?'

'That's right.'

Marley moved aside so she was in the frame and he focussed. Through the lens she looked straight at him, and deep into him. It shocked him for a moment, that look. She knew what she was doing. Marley took the seat opposite her. He leaned over and extended his hand for a second time. This time she just nodded. He took it back and wiped it across his middle again.

'OK. So, great to finally meet you. Thank you so much. I was thinking of starting with the release of your first single but then really get on to your father. He was your manager right? To get started? Have you seen the questions?'

'Really?'

'Oh. Yes, well…'

He handed her a sheet. Her hands were pale and sharp in detail, an artist's sketch. Her lips pursed. She handed it back.

'No. I've never seen this.'

'Oh. Well, I sent them, well, weeks ago. Can you, um, is it OK?' He held it out to her again. 'Let's just go. Brady? Set?'

Brady closed in on her face. Something was emanating from her. Underneath the almost transparent skin, there in the angle of her cheekbones, the way her lips parted slightly, the turn of her neck, the tilt of her head, when a lock of hair slipped from its tie, hanging curled behind her ear, every movement was a close study of beauty but was coming through the lens was a force. Through the camera that beauty was transformed into a latent, pulsating sexuality.

She didn't take the paper. Sam Ju was by her side in a second, taking the page and starting to read. They began to speak in low tones. Marley was on the edge of his seat, his desperation perched.

'We can change what you want. I did send this to your management, but look, we can change…'

She looked at Sam Ju and he understood and straightened up, pushing his glasses back on his face. Brady saw she was going to stand. He could count the slow beat. Ten, nine…

'No, we're not going to do it today. We will have to review the questions.'

'Oh. But, wait, you said you had one hour. Can we…?'

Five, four…

'Thank you, Mr Crocker. We will be in contact.'

23

One.

She stood and looked directly into the camera, right into Brady. There it was. He felt a tugging deep inside him. The drag of a hook in his belly. Then she turned and walked to the door. The other man opened it for her.

Marley looked helpless. 'When? When will you...?'

'It will be soon, Mr Crocker. In the next few days. Now excuse us, thank you. We will be in contact.' Sam Ju followed Soraya from the studio.

Marley was left standing with the paper of questions in his hand, staring at the door. Then it opened again. Ping came through with two bottles of beer in each hand.

'She just... Is she gone? I didn't know...' then she stopped. Marley still didn't move. His mouth was dropping, his expression sliding again. Brady walked to other side of the studio and checked the locked off shot. Sixteen minutes.

He walked over and took one of the beers.

'This'll do. Thanks Ping.'

* * *

That night, Marley had Zero over. He'd stopped pretending it was for anything other than sex by the end of the second week and stopped trying to hide it from Brady. Zero always looked fresh, always smiled and gave a blink and a little nod. He wore slip on shoes without socks and soft linen trousers. The bell rang. Marley pressed the gate button and poured two glasses of wine. Brady opened the door just as Zero stepped out of the elevator. He blinked, smiled and nodded and Brady nodded too as they passed. Downstairs, the humid city air hit him, and he was sweating by the time he walked

24

to the front gate. The riverbank was busy. He could hear it. A rich babble of voices, boats' horns, a feeling of music flowing underneath. He was just about to take his camera out when his phone rang.

'Hello, Mr White? It's Sam Ju, I met you earlier today.'

Brady stepped back and looked up. From here he could see the apartment window. It was a wall of glass from floor to ceiling. All of the lights were on.

'Yes. Hello Sam Ju. What can I do for you?'

'Soraya wants to schedule another interview for tomorrow.'

'Excellent, thank you, I'll tell Marley…'

'Well, that's the thing Mr White, Soraya wants to do the interview with you.'

Brady sat down on the low wall. A clicking of insects mixed with road noise and the riverbank. Mosquitos hovered near the thick plants behind the wall. He slapped his neck and checked his hand. Missed.

'It's Marley, Mr Crocker, who is doing the interview. I'm just the camera man.'

'Even so, Soraya wants to do the interview with you. She doesn't want to meet Mr Crocker again. If you want these interviews, then it will be you she talks to, Mr White.'

'Well…'

'I will message you the details, Mr White.'

'Sam Ju, call me Brady.'

'Goodnight, Brady.'

And that was it. He looked up at the apartment again. The lights had dimmed. Zero would be dancing, maybe undressed by now. Marley would be wanking on the couch. Brady turned and walked onto the bridge.

* * *

This time of night, the pleasure boats cruised up and down the river. Each one cut a white trail in the dark water, then the trail disappeared. On the bank, an elderly group counted steps in couples and slowly stepped out a ballroom dance. The passing boats were covered in lights running and flashing along the sides, and couples were dancing in them too. Up on the bridge the traffic passed quickly, rush after rush after rush mixing with the beat music from the slow boats drifting and the big band foxtrot from the old speakers on the bank. Brady took some shots of the reflections on the water, but couldn't capture the chaos of sound in the frame. He closed his camera then walked to the other side and headed for Mulligans.

English speakers clustered around this place like flies. Colette was there. Her spot was at the end of the bar, and every night she was hit on by at least one guy who fancied his chances with a tall dark-skinned French girl. Colette brushed them all off, though Brady knew she enjoyed the attention. He sat next to her.

'Anything?' she asked.

He put his cigarettes and phone on the bar. 'Yeah, well more delays, but you know.'

Colette gestured as if tossing handfuls of flour into the air around her. 'Ugh. This whole place is one delay after another. Another day, another day. How does anything get done?' She leaned over and took a cigarette from his pack. Colette was a dancer who said she'd been brought over to participate in a poetry-through-dance arts programme. The first time they met she spent forty minutes explaining to Brady how by bringing symbolic dance and symbolic words together, inaccessible truth could be accessed and the inexpressible could be expressed. Now she spent every night after rehearsal at the bar, expressing to Amy, the bar-lady, how inept everyone was and what a waste of her talent this project was.

Now Amy put a beer in front of him. 'How's the family back home?'

Something tugged at Brady's throat, and he felt sick. 'We keep missing each other. The time difference. So it's just messages.'

At first, there were several messages a day. Now it was a few a week.

'She's just getting used to you being away.'

'And the kids.'

'And the kids. I bet she's keeping them busy to keep their minds off how much they miss you.'

Brady picked up his bottle. 'Thanks Amy.' His phone buzzed.

'You see? There you go.'

It was from Sam Ju, detailing the venue and time for the next day. You don't need anyone else, it said. Soraya just wants to talk to you. He replied, OK. Then typed a message to his wife. Looks like stuff is finally starting to happen x x. Colette was talking again. When she exhaled the smoke, she lifted her chin and blew a thin stream into the air. The beer was bitter and cold. Outside, a line of suited businessmen passed in single file. Bikes went by. A man walking a giant huskie put on a plastic glove while waiting for his dog to finish shitting.

* * *

The directions led Brady deep into the city. Here the roads were narrower, the walls and the streets were pushed together without a plan. Newer shops and flats were built on the old, a mismatch of age and colour, and creeping vines spread from the corners over the buildings like veins on the outside of a dull skin. Along an avenue was a huge courthouse outside of which stood four guards, holding guns and wearing helmets. When Brady showed them his ID they checked through his bags before they allowed him through to the next gate. Sam Ju appeared.

'Welcome Mr White–'

'Brady.'

'Brady, sorry. Soraya is waiting for you, it's this way.'

'Why won't she meet with Marley?'

'Brady, she is very particular about who she comes in contact with. I'm sure you can appreciate that, given her circumstances. She is the best-selling artist in the country. Practically every teenage girl has her album, and her poster on their wall. She is a national role model. The wrong kind of person could put that in danger, put them in danger, Brady. Tell me, have you listened to her music? Have you seen her films?'

'I've heard the songs.'

'They speak to millions of children and young people, every day. It means a lot to them. She means a lot to them. We have to consider not just Soraya but the children too. It's very real.'

They walked through the corridors until they came to another door and two big men standing silently. Inside, the room was sparse and filled with light, Soraya was at a side table pouring a drink. Her hair was down, the tight braids from the day before were gone, her dress was long and loose, and her feet were bare. When she turned, she smiled.

'Good timing. A drink Brady?'

'Perfect.'

'You can set up, I thought we'd do it with the courtyard in the background.'

Sam Ju moved across the room and opened double doors, and an ornate courtyard was revealed with statues and hanging plants, a calm in the craziness of the city centre. Brady circled the room before setting his bags down.

'Yeah, we won't need the lights, this is it. With the courtyard behind.'

Soraya walked across with his drink. It was a strong dark brandy. The taste ran through him like a slow electricity. He waited for it to fill him in the same way he saw the sunlight fill the room before he started to take test shots. In this light he could see the sleek contours of her body through the dress, and for an instant imagined it slipping from her shoulders and how the light would glow on her skin. She glanced up at him through the lens. He settled on a spot. Sam Ju moved a seat into the room and set it in front of him.

'Is that OK? Do you have a script Brady?'

'Have you still got your copy of Marley's questions?'

'You're not going to use those?'

'So that I know what not to ask.'

Sam Ju nodded and left the room. Brady took another sip and set the camera.

* * *

The afternoon passed easily; the light washed around the bright room. The hanging green vines in the courtyard, just out of focus, swayed slowly. The rhythm of traffic and the rustling of city movement was a hypnotic score and Soraya's voice glided over it all as she went through her dreams and disappointments of youth, the ecstasy and confusion of sudden stardom. The scale of it had

29

removed her from any kind of normality. Her life would never be normal again. Brady let her talk, nudging the conversation along when it slowed. When the light started to turn away, they stopped.

'We're getting somewhere.'

'I'll let Sam Ju know when we'll do more.'

He started to put the camera away.

'And you Brady? What about you? What should we know about you?'

'Well, ask me a question.'

She smiled and stood, then slowly took her glass to the side table and filled it again. By the time she turned around he had zipped his bag and straightened up.

'Well, thanks. I'll go. I'll see you soon.'

'Oh, yes. Well, Brady. See you soon.'

When he stepped outside on to the street again he was straight into the heat and the noise, the thickness of this place, the closeness of the constant movement through the canyons of concrete, the millions of lives teeming in the early evening, all scraping against each other, all going somewhere. He'd been there for four weeks.

* * *

When he got back to the apartment, Zero was still there. This had never happened before. Zero always left before morning with a gentle pad to the door, a pause and a breath as he put on his shoes and slowly closed the door. But now Zero was sitting at the table, eating from a plastic box, wearing only his boxer shorts. He smiled.

'Brady. Brady! I'm not dressed! So sorry, and it's not the night, still day! You look younger in the day.'

'So do you, Zero. Every time I see you. But the day's nearly over.'

30

'I didn't get enough for two. Marley doesn't want to eat and I didn't know…'

'No problem Zero, I'll eat at Mulligans. Marley's asleep?'

'Well, resting maybe.'

Brady checked his phone as he spoke. No messages. 'D'you want to come for a drink?'

'Oh. To Mulligans? I've never been.' Zero cocked his head to the side while he stirred his noodles. 'Um, I think I will stay here. Marley will wake up soon I think.'

'It's a good place Zero, you should come by sometime.'

Zero looked up again and smiled. Brady turned and left. The evening air was heavy and by the time he crossed the river to Mulligans, a layer of the city was stuck to him. Colette was at the bar with a tall well-dressed man whose tie was done up all the way. Her and Brady's eyes met, but she didn't acknowledge him, just slid her eyes off him and continued blowing thin streams of smoke into a cloud above the man's head as he talked eagerly. Brady sat at the bar. Amy put a beer in front of him.

'Gonna eat?'

'We'll see. Thanks Amy. Does she ever go home with any of these guys?'

Amy shrugged.

'Just seems there's always guys around her, telling her their stories, asking about hers,' he said.

'It's a big city. There are lots of guys.'

'Doesn't she get tired of telling them all the same thing?'

'Oh come on, Colette is alright.'

'How about you Amy?'

'Ha,' she wiped the counter and looked up as a group of five entered the bar. They wore baseball hats and sports jackets with slogans and were peering at the drinks menu, pointing and nodding. 'This place. That's me. This is a holding pen. Really, that's it.' She shrugged again, and went to serve them. Brady checked his phone. No messages.

* * *

The next day, Soraya wore the same loose dress. The morning light in the room made Brady think of a chapel.

He said, 'How about relationships?'

'Personal relationships?'

'Yes. Not business.'

'Because business is still relationships. You're still with people and their emotions, their hang-ups, their…'

'OK, yes. Not business.'

'Family?'

'No. I guess what I mean is, what about love? Is there room for that?'

She lifted her hands as if in prayer, smiled and then gave a little applause.

'Love,' she said. 'Love is so hard to separate…' She stood. Every time she walked to the corner table, her hips swayed through the thin fabric. Her steps and the small swing of her arms had a cadence of visual poetry. From the table she selected a bottle and poured two glasses.

'Water, Brady? From the mountains. From high in the mountains. The purest.' She put the glass in front of him. 'OK. Let's talk about love.'

* * *

Sliding over the morning, skimming the time with sips from the water, Soraya talked about love and money. The status of power, or perceived power that success had granted, was an intimidation to men. Either they tried to assert themselves too much or they bent like saplings and were too weak. Her money, her fame, pushed them around. There was no balance. It was all too messy. Love was an impossibility. She wished she could put the whole thing down, just for a night, and see who she would meet. Whose eye she'd catch at the bar, whose look would make her flush and look away, but take a quick glance back, and see that he had flushed too. That's how it happens, right? But no. So, she felt lonely. She supposed she had gotten used to it. Brady could feel himself slipping away. He stood and stopped the camera.

'I'm going to need some food soon. I haven't eaten.'

'I'll call Sam Ju.' She walked to the counter again and spoke into her phone. He checked his. No messages. When she sat down again, she said, 'I'm sorry Brady, I must say, that you've been so long waiting for this.'

'Well, you know. I've got lots of city footage.'

'What do you think of it?'

'Huge. Busy. Rich. Poor. There's a lot.'

'A lot?'

'Of stories, I guess.'

'Stories. Is that why you do it? With a camera?'

'Everybody's just trying to get on. So everybody's got their own.'

'You have a ring, Brady. I want to ask you, do you treat your wife well?'

Brady wondered when the food was going to arrive. His head was starting to fill with light.

'Not well enough.'

'No?'

'Yes, I'm sorry, look, I didn't eat breakfast. I'm–'

Sam Ju entered pushing a table of food. The thick smell of broth and rice and fried meat flooded the room. Without saying a word, he gave a quick nod, turned and

33

left. As they started to eat, she said, 'We can talk more later. I'd like to do more, if you want. You can follow me. Come and see what's in my life. I can get an extension on your visa. Let's talk online. What's your username?'

* * *

Marley was out when the call came through. He answered and she was there on video call, in his hand. The light around her was different. She was in a different room.

'Are you alone?' her voice echoed slightly.

'Yes.'

'Are you sure?'

'Yes, it's just me in the apartment. In my room.'

'Have you been thinking of me? I've been thinking of you.' She stepped back from the screen and sat on the edge of a bed. She was wearing only a transparent negligee and panties. 'Let's make some time. Take your clothes off. Join me.'

His body froze and his mind opened, and everything rushed in, like a big river, heavy and swirling and filling the space inside him like a dam.

'I don't know if…'

'I do. I know how you look at me through the camera Brady. I can feel it. Your eyes on me. Am I right? I know I'm right. Let's just make each other happy for a little while. Tell me what you'd like.'

He undressed, watching her all the while, transfixed by this magnet of sexual energy running her hands over her body, encouraging him to show himself.

'Are you safe, doing this?'

'We know who we are. Tell me what you would do to me if I was there with you.'

He started hesitantly, but concentrated, struggling with the swirling heavy waters clearing a flood plain and slowly, determinedly, he pushed it all away, forced it all back until there was space for this, and even more, until this was the only thing there was. They talked in whispered breathy tones, but as the fever built, they were encouraging each other to a higher intensity, telling each other to go further, both of them pushing the world further and further away, until they were shouting over one another, their fever ballooning, stretching the sides, creating more space inside for more forgetting. When he was spent, he looked at his hands and the sheets and the floor. 'I've got to get cleaned up.'

She replied, 'Well, I'll see you tomorrow.' and she was gone. The heat was still inside him. He heard the click of Marley's door closing. His heart was still thudding. His phone pinged.

I have a minute now. How is it? Any date yet?

He went to the bathroom and washed his face. He gathered some tissue and wiped the floor and the bedsheets, then sat on the edge of the bed. He slowed his breathing and called.

'Hiya. How are you doing babe?'

'Oh its nuts. And cold, really cold. You know. But we're good. What about you?'

'How are the boys?'

'They're good. Driving me crazy.'

'Has Joey taken off his catcher's mitt yet?'

'What? Oh, the mitt. Yeah, that's forgotten about now. He doesn't want to go to practice anymore. Yeah, he's causing a fuss alright.'

'And Al?'

'He's on his phone all the time. Like it's a prayer book.'

Brady could hear her cutting something and then putting something on the counter. Maybe the lid of a jar. Toast?

'Well, tell him to message me. If he's on it all the time.'

'I will. What about you? Your visa is nearly up. Are you getting an extension?'

She bit into something. Toast.

'The interview has started at last. Things are beginning to happen. I don't know, I might need one.'

'How long?'

'I don't know. Jesus, not long I hope.'

There was the sound of something dragging and a puff of breath.

'Are you OK?'

'Yeah, I'm just putting a wash on. It's just…' Another heavy breath. 'There. What's she like?'

'OK, I think. She seems alright. She doesn't mind talking.'

'Even though she's been jerking you around since day one?'

'Look, it's the management. Hey, can we videocall?'

'Right. The management. Is there anyone else? Have you found yourself another reason to stay? Someone else worth staying for?'

'Come on. Of course not.'

'Not that that means anything.'

'Yes, it does. It's the management. It is. Look, at least things are moving. Started. It means I can finish and come back. Can we videocall?'

'Brady, I'm doing a hundred things here. You're on speaker.'

Another sigh. Something being closed. Another crunch of toast.

'Look, I don't know exactly when I'll be back and…
I feel like… I feel like inside it's just a desert. You know?
Just a desert. With nothing. Like I've made it myself, and
there's nothing there. Nothing's there, nothing can grow
until I get back to you. I just don't know when that's
going to be.'

There was no sound now, nothing from the other
side. He pressed the phone to his ear, pushing to try and
hear something. Silence.

'Are you there?'

'I don't know what to do with that Brady. What do
you want me to do with that? You're right, you did make
it. I don't know what you want me to say. Every time
you build something up, you knock it down again. It
keeps happening. It's inevitable. Al's got service at five
and I'll need to feed them straight from school. Good
luck with the interviews. I hope she's interesting enough
for Marley's documentary.'

'Ah come on… just… just tell the boys I said hi and
I love them and that it won't be long now.'

'OK, I will.'

'OK.'

'I've got to go.'

These four simple words fell into the room, and into
him, like stones, huge heavy stones thudding onto the
desert earth right down in the pit of his stomach.

He said, 'Bye.'

She said, 'Bye.'

He slumped onto the edge of bed, unable to move.

* * *

The next morning, the light in the room had changed, a
heavy cloud was over the city, and the humidity was
intense. When he arrived, her demeanour was the same

as the day before, as if nothing had happened. He felt on edge, as if at any second, someone was going to come and take him away. He checked the light meter and looked around.

'It's darker. Let's do a mood change,' he said. 'How about you change your dress, I'll set up my lamps.'

When she returned, she was wearing a loose shirt and combat pants. She smiled, then pursed her lips and sat down. He pressed record. She hardly spoke, but then neither did he. Brady asked her questions and said, 'tell me about…' but her replies faded like the boat trails in the river. He let them go and allowed the recorder to hear the shuffling in the seats, the pad of feet to and from the cabinet, drinks on the table, he let the camera see her look into space then land her eyes on him, then off again. Her delicate features, the way her lips turned up to her coy smile and her eyes so demure, she was a model of sublime beauty, but all he could think about now was her lying on the bed with her legs apart, groaning and telling the camera what she wanted to feel. Questions floated through him, but he didn't voice them, it didn't seem worth it. He didn't want to pick up and sift through answers. The afternoon came around, slowly.

'Mistakes. What have your biggest mistakes been?'

'Mistakes. I don't think about it. I don't think mistakes matter so much when you're alone.'

'Then do you make more of them, if they don't matter so much?'

'When you're alone who's to say they're mistakes? If they don't affect anyone?'

'OK. This will be the last session, I think.'

'You want to go? You don't like China, Brady?'

'I need to leave.'

He pressed stop on the camera.

'Brady you have to stay. We can continue. You are going to follow me. Exclusive access.'

'How can you have trusted me for that? Surely you know how vulnerable you made yourself.'

'I think I know you. I think you know me. I'm not vulnerable. Now I think maybe you are. Let's start again, let's keep talking. I like you Brady. Can't we just have something simple? Look. Let's keep going. It's simple. We've got this, and we've got what happened last night. You're going back when this finishes. Let's keep going, I want to talk.'

He pressed record. She sat opposite him. Now he couldn't think of a single question. There was nothing left. The space that was created within him, that plateau cleared, all of his life pushed aside would never be filled again. Not by her, not by anyone. How to drive love from your heart.

She started to talk about her father. He'd supported her throughout her childhood, with love, and was her manager when she was a teenage star. Once she surpassed a particular point of success, once it was clear that the money coming in could make him a millionaire, she stopped being a daughter to him and he did everything he could to exploit this commodity. He was clever and cruel. Her songs, her image, were ubiquitous and her whole life was designed to perpetuate and increase the revenue. He was obsessed with the scale of it. Gaining great wealth in a country like this was like moving a planet. When she was old enough, she fired him. Brady relaxed back into the task. It was easy to sit here and let this impossibly beautiful woman talk about an impossibly rapid accumulation of wealth and fame. So he let her talk. The subject came back around to the impossibility of love and any kind of normal relationship.

'OK. OK. When we spoke about love, yesterday, you said you'd never been in love because it's unattainable because of who you are, because of your situation. But don't people fall in love regardless? It's not really a choice. Love, surely, is not a choice. Has is it ever happened whether you wanted it to or not?'

'No. Brady. That's in songs for teenagers. Love is a choice. Lust is not.'

He didn't say anything. The camera kept recording.

* * *

As soon as he got in the apartment, he took his shoes off and went straight to the fridge. He stood at the window and drank his beer. Through the glass were endless pinnacles of light, tips of neon. Projections and LEDs made designs on the towering buildings across the skyline. Here were diamonds and spirals, here was the silhouette of a dancing woman, here was a gymnast morphing into a doctor, into a boxer, into a construction worker, into a pop star. The bridge across the river drew beads of light, making six bands of white and red, the city pulling two ways. Down on the river front people walked, danced, jogged. Some were taking pictures across the river, some had stopped to listen to a Karaoke singer. He went to the fridge again for a fresh beer and then sat on the sofa looking out at the endless city.

Marley arrived. Brady watched his big grotesque reflection come through the door, walk in and stand behind the chair. Brady lifted his arm and shook his empty beer can.

'You can get me one if you're getting one.'

They looked at each other in the dark glass.

'You absolute shit. You've fucked me over. My gig, and you–'

'Woah. Marley. I'm working on the project. Your project. Your project is getting done because she wants to talk to me. I didn't ask her.'

'How much have you got?'

'About twelve thirty. And it's all yours.'

'In one day?'

'Three.'

'Three? You didn't tell me?'

Brady stood and turned. Marley's face was screwed up. 'I'll get one myself then.' He came back with two and put one in Marley's hand before sitting down again.

'Why does she want to talk to you? This place makes me fucking sick.'

'What about Zero?'

'What about Zero? Fuck Zero. Zero's only around because I'm paying him.'

'I wouldn't be here if I wasn't getting paid.'

'Fuck you too.'

They both opened the beers. From up here, the boats moved slowly. From up here, the river was a thick slow dark artery.

'Well, I think I'm through.'

'You can't be through, you dickhead. You've just started. You've just got what we came here for.'

'What you came here for.'

'If you leave now, I'm fucked Brady. You haven't put everything on the line for this. Don't do it to me. You can't go now, we've just got it.'

'I'm going for a drink.'

* * *

Mulligans was deserted. The tables were empty and Amy was wiping the bar, singing gently to herself. She poured a beer when she saw Brady and put it on the bar as he sat down.

'I was going to close early. Look at it.'

'Kitchen closed?'

'Ah, yes. Hungry?'

'Don't worry, I'll get something from up the road.'

'Well… no. Let me close first and then I'll put something on for the two of us.'

Brady sipped his beer while Amy closed the glass doors. Then she went into the kitchen. Now the street noise was blocked out, he listened to the humming of the fridges, the high pitch of the AC, the gentle clinking from the kitchen, and Amy's soft voice running over a chorus again and again until she came out and smiled.

'It won't be long.' She pulled herself a beer and came out from behind the bar. They sat at a table.

'Amy, thank you. You're always so good. And I've never heard you sing before.'

'That's not what I'd call it.'

'Oh, come on, a true talent. How about Karaoke after?'

Amy laughed and drank some beer.

'They do it, you know, on the riverfront in the mornings. It wakes me up. Have you seen it?'

'No. I don't do mornings. I'm never out of this place before three. Except tonight maybe.'

'Well, tonight let me take you for a drink. Somewhere nice. The rooftop at the park.'

'That would be nice. No Karaoke.'

'Promise. No Karaoke.'

There was a timer ping from the kitchen. Amy excused herself. The low light reflecting off the unlit table lamps, the glass partitions of the booths, the mirror behind the bar, the glass doors closed to the street, made this place feel like being inside a jewel. Amy came out carrying two bowls of noodles in fresh soup.

'You don't have your camera,' she said, setting them down.

'No. I didn't know this was on the menu.'

'Nobody comes here for noodles. They come here for what they get at home.'

She sat opposite him.

'Any news on going home?'

He shrugged. 'I want to get back to the kids.'

'And your wife.'

'Yes. Though I'm not sure she wants me to.'

'Oh. She doesn't want you back?'

Brady shook his head.

'Maybe she's angry? About you going away?'

'She has plenty of reasons to be angry.'

'Oh. How's the filming?'

'Good, at last. We've got to the interview.'

'How is that? What's she like?'

'She's nice. She doesn't like Marley. I'm just asking questions.'

'No one likes Marley. Sorry. Is she answering your questions?'

'People don't really answer questions, do they? They just find ways to say what they want to say. Or else it's just silence. And you can put your own answers into a silence.'

When they finished, Amy took their bowls back into the kitchen and went behind the bar. She selected two thin glasses and set about looking for a particular bottle. Brady took his phone out. Amy sat down and placed the glasses in front of them.

'You're staying for a while then?'

'It's a choice.'

'Well, this is from the mountains. It's a firewater. Sip it.'

'There's a blues and jazz trio at The Rooftop tonight. You like that kinda thing, right?'

'Sounds great.' They clinked glasses. A movement at the window caught Brady's eye. It was someone cupping their hands against the glass, peering in. Colette. There were other shapes too, moving around behind her. She knocked. Brady could hear the muted sound of her calling Amy and the hubbub of laughter.

'Colette,' he said.

'And her theatre group. It was the premiere tonight. I didn't think they'd come back here.'

'Are you going to open?'

Amy swallowed the glass in one, then took the ring of keys from her pocket and walked to the door singing the chorus again and shaking her head. When she got to the door, she turned and looked at Brady. 'It would have been nice. Thanks anyway.'

Brady swallowed his drink too and it burned through him as the theatre group rolled in and all of the noise rolled with them, actors and dancers and costume designers, choreographers and directors, all tumbling together towards the bar, an ejaculation of self-congratulatory achievement splashing into the room.

'Oh Brady!' Colette exclaimed, 'You would have loved it! Oh, what a show! Everyone, this is Brady, he is working the camera on a project about Soraya.' Oohs and aahs floated up into the air. 'Everybody loves him, don't we Amy? What shall we have? Champagne? Amy?'

'She was just about to go. We were just about to go,' he said, but people had already turned to the bar, and Amy was there, preparing glasses, opening bottles and the bar was lined. He went to her side and took orders, poured drinks, found the music playlist she wanted. He kept filling two little shot glasses with the firewater and putting one in Amy's hand. The two of them would clink and swallow and return to serving. As he was making sure the doors were closed and the lights outside were off, he saw the little man walking his giant huskie and behind him was Zero coming up the street, looking at the names of the bars as he passed them. Brady stepped out. Zero saw him and smiled and waved.

'I found you!'

'Come on in,' Brady said. 'It's a bit of a party. I'll introduce you.'

Zero squinted through the glass. 'Who are they? What do they do? What should I say I do?'

'I can introduce you. Just say that you work for Soraya. As an assistant, but if anyone asks you about her, say you can't say anything, nothing at all. You'll be fine.'

He looked at his reflection in the glass and ran his fingers through his hair and straightened his shirt. 'So that's who I am?'

'No, come on. It's just a story about you. These are theatre people, they'll buy into a good story.' Zero didn't say anything, just stood at the door and scanned the room.

'Unless you want to tell them? I guess Zero, it depends on what you want from them, what story you tell.'

'OK, I'll come in, thank you.'

'I'll get you a drink. Then it's up to you.'

Brady closed the door behind them and instantly, talk of the show and symbolism and ground-breaking collaborations and the essences of art spun around their heads while underneath, people were touching and seducing, complimenting and promising. Zero was absorbed into the cloud of theatre. The more drink was poured, the longer the hands stayed, the closer the promises became. Later, from behind the bar, Brady saw him drinking champagne while a director stood close to him, animated with theatrical zeal, as a flamboyantly dressed set designer refilled his glass. His phone beeped. It was a message.

Are you alone? I am. X.

Brady looked up. There was a shadow at the door, and Amy went to open it. It was Marley. He looked in over Amy's head and then Brady saw his big unhappy form turn and walk away. Amy closed the door and came behind the bar.

'Is he OK?' she said.

'I thought you didn't like him.'

'I don't, but…'

Brady handed her another firewater. 'This isn't going to end soon,' he said.

'No,' she said. They clinked glasses again. Colette started singing in a falsetto with her eyes closed and some dancers started swirling around her. On the other side of the room, the director was even closer to Zero, now telling him about roles and positions, how much truth there is within the live performance, how the camera will never replace actually seeing the thing happen before you. The camera changes the narrative. The camera makes a lie.

Outside, the city night was humid. The pleasure boats had stopped now, the garish projections on the buildings were off, the music on the bank was gone and the big river rolled millions of dark tonnes of water under the bridge. Unstoppable. Inevitable.

POISON

By now, Cabo looked like all of his colleagues in the Grand Parliament building – except, of course, for the stick. Nobody else walked with a stick like his. But Cabo, unlike his colleagues, came from a poor family, from a troubled birth in a high mountain village. Born strong, stronger than his mother as it turned out. Then, after the birth it was just him and his father. His father kept a little fried food shack, until one night he lost control of his car and came off the wrong side of the steep road. If he hadn't drunk so much, he wouldn't have lost control, but anyway there was a tumour creeping through his brain that would have finished him within a year. Cabo was fourteen. There was no war then.

Seth and Anka took Cabo in. Because, Seth said, he was going to train to be a priest, and, well, it was a very Christian thing to do, to take in an orphan. Cabo worked in a little bar and saved his money under a floorboard in his room in a buckled house balanced on the hill. It had a crooked stairs, loose windows and holes in the doors where Seth's fist came through when the passion of the lord overtook him. Seth said religious life was like the mountain road – the wrong side was a long way down. The white winters could be brutal, freezing the hillside still, but in the summer the mountain was pressed between the heat pushing down and the humidity rising up and everything grew green and grew fast, and the creaks and clicks and songs and whirrs and snaps of life burst out across the peaks.

During the months of heat, Cabo and Seth took to walking through the forest, stepping their way down in the fast freezing waters of the shallow rocky river. Seth cut sturdy oak sticks to help them keep balance. He'd stop during the day to pray. He found a place where he felt the light. It was a clearing in the trees near the bank. Here, the birdsong came from every direction and the undergrowth of the forest was illuminated from the inside, the colours were coming up from underneath, out of the fresh shoots and flowers and the glowing rich green moss. Seth would stop and pray, and Cabo would stand in the river in a hollow where the icy running water pooled nearly up to his knees. It was very beautiful, Cabo agreed, just like how he imagined a piece of heaven to be. One day, after prayer, further down the river when Cabo told Seth that he wanted to save money so he could go to school, Seth stopped him and said that he too would be saving money, but for a church.

'What would you do with school anyway?'

'Get a job. Go to the city. Work in the city.'

'Serving who?'

'Serving?'

'Everyone serves somebody Cabo. Who will you serve? I will serve the Lord, and he will provide. I will gather a church here in this mountain and together we will provide. Then you won't have to go to the city. What you want will be here. The church will bring everyone together and we will provide for each other, because the Lord will be with us. His bounty, his endless bounty will be bestowed upon us.'

The passion was in him then, and he raised his voice in sermon to the trees. He lifted the stick and shook it as he spoke. 'By coming together and devoting to God we shall remain virtuous, worthy of his blessing. God provides and keeps his followers penitent and pure. God keeps his followers upright and saves them from falling into sin, into hell. He will keep us from falling, from being swept away by sin! We will be upright and strong. Like this stick!!' he shouted to the forest and struck it victoriously into the air. Cabo sat down on the bank and said that he could keep the stick, he just needed money.

* * *

When they came across the bones on the riverbank, Seth guessed it was a forest rat, but it seemed too big. They couldn't decide. Still, the skull looked like a rat's. In the hot summer woods around the river, Cabo saw plenty of death. The more life there is, the more death there is, he supposed. In Seth's circle of sunlight, something had killed a bird. There was a scattering of bright feathers, colours ripped and discarded, lit like the dawn over the village street after the summer carnival. Whatever had eaten it had devoured the body, bones and all, and left the wings – its sky blue and white feathered wings – which lay open on either side of its missing body, spread in a gruesome empty welcome. They both stood in the pool of ice water staring at where the bird's body should have been, when Cabo stepped on something that moved. He felt a bite on his heel and lost his balance, and fell backwards into the water. The snake was gone before either of them could see it.

* * *

The doctor said that by the size of the bite, the snake must have been more than a metre long. Cabo was lucky, it could have been much worse, he said, but the poison was strong. Back at the crooked house he took the medicine, but the dizziness and sickness didn't fade. Anka brought him soups and tried to help him sit up and eat, but he couldn't respond, he was a ghost in his delirium. The worst was the fever. Seth prayed for him but the fever was a fire inside him and Cabo was weakened. He was being hollowed, and had neither been asleep nor awake for days when Seth took the sheets, and the pillows, and the chair, and his clothes, and the closet and the posters and the pictures, and burned them all at the back of the house. The smoke crept up the mountainside, like a huge black leopard stalking prey. Seth said it was the Devil leaving. Cabo started to come around. He was able to eat and, at last, he was able to sleep.

When he finally went back to the river, Seth presented him with a new oak stick. He had cut three grooves into the end of it and into these he'd inserted stones, thinned and sharpened by the river. The stones were tied with rope. The stick was a little axe now.

'You see, now we have weapons instead of walking sticks. Another snake and, bang!' said Seth and he swung his stick in an arc. It splashed the water and stuck into the riverbed. Cabo took his stick and wandered back up along the bank. He found the animal skull. He sat cross-legged on the bank and untied the rope and fixed the bone into the middle groove on the point of the stick. Then he went to the glowing prayer circle where the wings lay.

He took the wings to the river. The protruding bones were thin, like fingers of an old man. He cleaned them, then connected the wings to the other two grooves in the head of the stick, then retied the rope to the head of the stick. He went back to the river. Seth was there with his axe-stick in his hand.

'Not a weapon anymore. It has a different kind of power. Imagine what I can be now.'

'Cabo, look at you, you still have a fever you fool. Now it's just a stick again. And we know now that the river isn't safe. How will you defend yourself, tickle the beast with your feathers?'

Cabo pushed Seth, and Seth pushed Cabo back. They gripped and pushed each other and then they were fighting, rolling in the running water of the cold cold river, scraping on the rocks, until Seth had Cabo by the neck and turned him over with all his weight on him and with his hand on the back of his head, pushed him into the water. Cabo struggled and squirmed, but Seth held him there. The water was violent then, the bubbles and submerged shouts of horror were taken downstream as Cabo thrashed. Seth was shaking and sweating with the cost of holding Cabo, but he pressed and pressed him down until at last, Cabo stopped fighting. He let him go and Cabo reared up and drew in breath like a titan breathing for the first time. Seth staggered out of the water and they slumped on the riverbank, both breathless.

'Did you want to drown me?'

'No, you fool… to fix the fever. For the poison. Push the poison out. Clean you. A baptism.'

* * *

It was this story that secured him the position of Assistant to the Defence Ambassador in the Parliament Building. The President was a deeply religious man. By then, the war was in its fifth year. There were a lot of deaths. Well, there was a lot of life. Though the daily dead weren't enough to cause much alarm, small numbers for long enough just strengthened the chain and provided more reasons to avenge and attack again.

The story of the stick arose as he was leaving the interview. The President stopped him just as he pushed the door to leave and asked him, 'Your stick. Where did you get your stick?'

Cabo let the door close again. He held it in front of him as he walked back to the table. After so many years, the wood was now dark and the skull was yellow and smooth, the feathers, still blue, stuck out on either side. He related the story of his childhood, the mountains, his sickness and his baptism. As soon as he left, the President and his colleagues nodded their heads and agreed that Cabo was the one who must take this role. Within days, he was entering negotiations with diplomats and treading the discreet line of assertion and deference. It was all about territory. All about resources. Who could lose the most. Who could last the longest.

* * *

Now, as he walked down the snow covered steps of the Grand Parliament Building against the white and blue street into the city evening, Cabo saw a shape he recognised. Seth was across the road, hooded and wearing loose clothing. He held his arms around himself, hugging his hands in the cold. Cabo stepped down and Seth came to him and opened his arms. He was bloated, and reddened as he exclaimed, 'Cabo, Cabo!'

They embraced. Seth smelled of sweat and old wool.

'Do you know it has been twenty years?'

'Twenty-four years.'

'Yes, twenty-four. You still hold the stick. It's kept well. My goodness. The skull and feathers…'

'Still strong Seth. What brings you here?'

Seth stepped back and pulled his coat around him again. He blew into his hands. Cabo saw that his skin was mottled a crimson and pink, purple at the edges, beneath his chin and between his fingers. Maybe he was ill or malnourished, but then again, it was very cold.

'I've come for a favour. I need your help Cabo. It's my son. I have a son, and he wants to leave the country, to fight, to join an army and fight.'

'What can I do?'

'You can tell him about it, talk to him. I don't want him to go. Anka and I have begged and pleaded with him.'

'Come with me. It's so cold, we'll go to my apartment. There's snow coming again.'

* * *

As they walked through the streets, heavy snow started to fall thick through the light and Seth told Cabo about his son. Eden was a bright boy, and from when he was young, his intelligence was commented upon with delight by everyone who met him. But the town was poor and Eden was frustrated, and his intelligence had turned to anger. He had started to fight. In the school and in the workplace, he would challenge anyone but was often beaten, coming home with cuts on his eyes and a bloodied mouth. Another lesson. But he didn't want to learn. He wanted to fight.

The cloud covering the city kept the light in, everything was touched on the inside with a quiet ghostly blue. Couples walked past, linked at the arm, snow on their hats and shoulders. When they came to the apartment building the glass doors slid aside and a gust of wind swirled snow around them as they stepped in.

'Come on, let's use the stairs,' Cabo said.

Seth was wheezing by the time they got to the fourth floor, his squeezed breathing echoing up the stairwell.

'Much further?' He stopped to take breath.

'I'm on twelve. Come on,' Cabo replied.

When they reached the apartment, Seth was sweating. Cabo took off his coat and put his stick in the corner. The apartment was poised on the edge of the city park and Seth could see all of it, laid out before him, covered in white.

'Do you live here alone?'

'I stay here in the week.'

Seth moved to the window and slowly got his breath back.

'The city looks so quiet in the snow. Oh lord, to look at it. The park is beautiful.'

Cabo moved to Seth, standing next to him at the window.

'Yes, look. When the snow is fresh, or is still falling, look how the park is laid out. It's not like the mountain, the ground doesn't disappear, you can see it. It spreads out, look. It's my favourite time when you can see the first tracks in the snow. The first animal prints.'

He pointed far below to where there was a track. Something had hopped or run across the grass, a line of dots across the white.

'See? I sometimes think they are like an instrument, a single instrument, you know? Like a violin maybe, or a clarinet, playing alone. See? One voice alone in the white silence. It breaks away from everything and makes its line. And it's never straight, that line.'

'I can't believe you still have the stick, Cabo.'

'Have you yours?'

'Goodness, no. No, of course not. The wood, the feathers. How did they last?'

'Oil. You know it, hazel oil. Vinegar. Just ordinary things.'

They stood side by side watching the falling snow drift down from the thick cloud. They watched it disappear down onto the park and cover up the animal track. There was a fountain in the middle. It had a spire on the top and its base was wide, surrounded by a halo of streetlights. The ice on the still water glinted now as the city dimmed.

Cabo turned and walked to the counter and poured two drinks.

'Seth, now tell me, how is your ministry?'

'No Cabo, I never had a ministry. I never left the village. I tried to make a church, but no one wanted God. No one wants to share. A church needs to share God. So me and Anka, we opened a shop. But now…'

He took the drink and sipped.

'Please. About my son.'

'What is it you want me to do Seth?'

'It's been so long Cabo and now here you are, look at where you are.'

'What is it you want him to do?'

'Oh, if we had money… but we have nothing. They'll take the house away from us you know. I already owe for my shop. They come and demand my earnings. If only we had some money, we could send him to a good school, we could let him see what else there is. He just needs to learn, my wife says. If he learns then he won't want to fight, that's what she says. Maybe she's right. If he has opportunity he won't want to fight.'

'So you came for money.'

Seth drank again and put the empty glass on the counter and stared at it painfully. His face slowly twisted into a grimace and then slowly released until it hung slack again.

He said, without lifting his eyes, 'Cabo, it feels terrible coming to you like this. Can you imagine? How I feel coming to you like this?'

'If he does go to fight, what if that's what he wants? Seth, if it were you and you were his age and wanted to do the same, would you let your parents stop you?'

'Dammit, Cabo, I can't just let him walk off to be killed. If he goes, he will be killed, won't he? It is war. You know. You see it. Could you send your boy away? And this is my son, my only son. Please. You must know how it hurts me to come to you like this. Look at me, look at me.'

He held his hands out. The ends of his sleeves were frayed, his skin was patched, the dull colour on his palms and fingers was broken and uneven.

'I have nothing in return, I have nothing to give you. Please. Help me.'

Cabo swallowed his drink, took his jacket from the stand and picked up the stick.

'Follow me.'

* * *

Seth followed him back down the canyon of the stairwell, panting as he took each step, and then they were outside in the cold again. Over the city, darkness had a hold and the snow took on a glow of slow magic falling. They walked into the park, with Cabo striding ahead and Seth following, his arms hugging his body, following the footprints and stick marks, adding a limping dragging echo to Cabo's staccato line straight to the fountain.

Cabo stood at the fountain and Seth caught up with him, his face distorted and his breath hurting him, stabbing him as he tried to stand straight again.

When he could speak, he said, 'Why are we here?'

Cabo held his stick high. The dull skull and blue-white wings pushed skyward, against the snowfall.

'Do you remember the animals?'

'Of course. It was, it was a forest rat, was it a rat? And the dead bird, the missing bird.'

'And the snake. The poison.'

'And the snake. We never saw the snake. It was in the water.'

'The water. Look now in the water. Here.'

'Cabo, please just help me. Look at me, can't you see?'

'Look in the water Seth.'

And so Seth did. He leaned over and peered into the water, trying to see underneath the skin of ice, looking for life in the darkness.

'There is nothing, what do you want me to—'

Then Cabo grabbed him from behind and pushed his head down and the ice broke, a crack echoed and in the thin transparent blue light, against the smooth stretched white of the city park, the two dark figures struggled at the base of the fountain. Cabo leaned on Seth, holding the stick across the back of his neck, pushing him down. The water shook and bubbled. The more Seth struggled, the tighter Cabo gripped, forcing him deeper. Still, Seth kept fighting, kicking his feet and pushing back, buckling and straining. Cabo gritted his teeth and pushed harder and harder until Seth went limp. The fight was over. Cabo pulled him out. Seth was bruised purple and blue and his mouth contorted, trying

57

to find a shape. Cabo dropped him and he writhed on his back, gasping and heaving huge painful lungfuls of cold air. His eyes were wild and rolling, as if looking at a great horror for the first time. Cabo crouched over him.

'Now you too are baptised Seth. Go home. Ask God about your son.'

He stuffed some notes into the wet crease of Seth's jacket, and turned and walked away. The snow had covered their tracks there and so he made a new one back – a pattern of threes across the smooth white.

A week later, Cabo was appointed Defence Minister. By then, Seth had made it back to the frozen mountains. Maybe he made it through to spring. The mountain winters can be brutal. The war goes on.

THE TALL OWL

Uncle Jack picked me up from the unit in his shaky old VW. We rattled along. Nobody washed this place. The city streets were worn and grimy, and not just the streets: the buildings, the railings, the windows, the river walls, the doorways, the signposts, the arrows, the traffic lights. I guess if it had something to live up to it might try. If there was some sense of itself, some city self-awareness, it might be shamed into cleanliness, but really it's like the guy on your street who goes for milk, unwashed, in his vest and shorts and socks; he just doesn't care. He's functioning isn't he? What more do you want? I don't know why I'd expected the city to have changed since I'd last been through it. Of course it hadn't. Kind of stupid of me.

I saw the owl as we passed in the car, for a second, in the corner of my eye. Just a glimpse, but I saw it – a giant bird stepping across the side street as we drove past, but now the side street and the bird were gone.

'Is there a parade or something?' I said.

'A parade? Today? No, no. Nothing in the city today. Why?'

He smiled at me. I didn't say anything.

'It's good to have you back.' He turned the CD player on and flicked through the track numbers, humming something. 'I picked up this new album. Well, it's an old album, but you know, new for me. Not for her, no, she's dead. This isn't new for her. The case is in the door next to you, have a look. She reminds me of you. I can imagine you doing her stuff. You've got that kinda voice.'

I had a look. This beautiful serious woman looked at me and leaned back on a car in front of an American diner. Very serious. She had someone to blame for it all. If the album wasn't a success, she could always be a juror, or maybe spend some time in a witness stand for prosecution, or she could just stare out of windows at passers-by, or sing at them through the glass. The principal remained the same. Bass tones' strings' plucks and belled piano drops floated into the air in the car and nudged me – and dammit, any second now her soft voice would be trying to get a song into me. Uncle Jack, looking at me, said, 'Oh. Are you listening to music?'

'Not yet.'

He switched it off and the air was safe again.

'When you start, you know, you should borrow it. I think you'd like it. Great lyrics too. You know, when you're ready. She's not going anywhere.'

I wanted to see it again, otherwise, well, otherwise it could have been a bump in the road, a digital glitch, a scratch on the CD, or a short circuit, a power surge, a magnetic response, an electrical fault, a feedback reflection – but yes, yes, I did see it again. At the next junction we were waiting for the lights to turn and it stepped out, right there in front of the cars. I'll describe it.

The owl is tall, taller than the car. Tall and white. There's a powder grey at the shoulders and the wings, and grey where the thin legs start, which bestow the odd look of a butler with orange amber eyes, but besides that, it's white – its body and glorious dignified face, with the thin feathery ridge that runs down to the beak which provides a singular symmetry, is beautifully, shimmeringly, white. On its feathers dance points of light upon the white like the sun on the wide water, like the spots of light skimming on the sea skin. Then there is the tremor of a constellation when the wind shifts and ruffles its plumage. It moves its head forward and back, in that odd detached way that owls do, with shoulders hunched, wings tucked politely at its side. Besides its noble beauty and awesome size, it is novel and friendly, like when a distant relative or your parents' friend who hasn't seen you for a while pops by to say hello but won't take their jacket off, they're just passing and they might have a treat or a little present for you, but they tell you you've grown and ask you how you are and what you're doing in school before they take their hands from their pockets.

Jack looked sideways at me. 'Everything alright?' The lights changed. He put the car in gear. The giant bird gave its wings a shake, throwing to the air shards of star, and when the line of cars started to move, it stood aside, its big legs and feet and talons stepping carefully off the road. Owls' talons are razor sharp for grabbing, holding and tearing, not for negotiating a café signboard on a small pavement.

'Who's going to be at the van?'

'Just Deb. Your Gran, obviously. I wouldn't be surprised if we get a few more. Some friends maybe, calling in. Some people have popped in over the last few days. Your Mum did say she'd like to come over, but it's up to you. I said I'd message her.'

We rolled slowly past it. It hunched and dipped its head and looked at me through the window. Owls' eyes are quite perfect, they're not flecked with different colours like ours. This one has a clean orange block colour surrounding its big black pupils, and the black of the pupil is absolutely black. It might even be the blackest thing I will ever see.

'Traffic's pretty good,' said Jack and he slid into another lane.

I looked in the side mirror. The bird's head was turned, but its body wasn't, owls are so strange – its big eyes looked at us as we drove away. Over my shoulder, out the back window I saw the wind ruffle its feathers again, and there was that shimmer, and a shape of light passed, whatever the opposite of a shadow is. Jack saw me and glanced in his rear-view mirror but didn't say anything. I faced forward again and looked at the street. Now Jack was humming quietly and tapping his hands on the wheel.

'Are you and Debbie still–?'

'Yup. Still apart. But we're back in the van since your Gran got bad. Your Gran is in hers. Deb spends every night there now, and takes care of her, well we both do, she can't do it herself. And she shouldn't. So she doesn't. I'm there, I sleep in ours and we do it together.'

'How bad is Gran?'

'Hmm. Well, pretty bad.' His eyes stayed on the road. 'You'll see. It's good that you've come out for a couple of days now. I really don't know how much longer she has. It is two days, right? That's how long you've got?'

We took a left onto the long curved road, to swing us away from the centre of the city.

'Would you like to do anything?'

'Just see Gran.'

Jack said, 'Well, anything else, just say, OK?'

I nodded. I looked out the side window up into the sky. Maybe I'd see it flying off.

He took a look at the sky too, looking where I was looking, then he smiled and slapped my leg gently. 'It's good to have you back Amy.'

* * *

Outside the city where the footpaths and road lights stop, beyond the shut down shops and boarded up libraries, the derelict public offices – that's where the caravan field is, right on the edge of the dirty fringe of the city. The fields are filled with old caravans, trailer vans, static vans, and mobile homes in haphazard rows. Some have little shelters or extra rooms stuck on the side, leaning wood or thin metal sheets banged together at post-disaster angles. There are a few diesel generators around the edge, linking up the vans with power, thick cables snaking over and under the uneven earth. There are parallel tracks, worn into the earth, stretching right down to the last row, and then they curve around and join up, so that you're coming back again. If you look down the lines of vans you can see the clothes lines, stretched and criss-crossing, and the old clothes bleed their old colours onto the last of the grass. Like those vintage black and white pictures of children in war zones, there's a beautiful grimness here. You'd know what I mean if you ever went in, if you took the right turn off the main road, but why would you? You only go places if there's something there you want, and there's nothing to get here. It doesn't lead anywhere. It's a disconnect. You only come in here if you live here, and if you live here, you only want to get out. You'd pass Sandy on the steps of her van, after the rain, sitting with her feet wide apart, in her apron and slacks, her elbow on her knees, sewing and stitching with pins in her mouth and the weight of her cruel vintage pulling her cheeks down from her eyes. But even that isn't enough to see, not really. Anyone can see that. Anyone could wander in, see Sandy there, take a picture and feel happy with themselves for capturing the authenticity, for spotting this vignette of poverty, but it isn't enough. If you'd seen her on that step day after day after day, all through my childhood, sewing and patching the clothes for us all for a few pennies a time, so that we didn't need to buy new; Sandy sitting and sewing thin melancholy into the fabric and pulling it tight, then you put those faded clothes back on, then maybe you'd start to understand. And when it's late like this, the thin van shells don't keep in the sounds of different tongues, television shows and radios and talk, murmurs and exclamations, and walking past one by one is like stepping through soft bundles of life. A rusted steel guitar strummed in a slow rhythm comes from a small van right at the end of our row. Old Archie. When the sun is shining, he brings out a battered creaky chair from his van and sits and plucks and strums the five strings of his beat-up guitar. He doesn't sing much, but when he does, it's a deep tuneless hypnotic baritone and the folk on the row come out to their doors or sit on their steps and listen. Something about the way he sings…his voice doesn't belong to him, it comes from inside whoever hears it. Straight away. If you heard it, you'd know. Even if you've never walked through these odd alleys, never waited inside your thin metal van for the rain to stop, never stopped on the tyre tracks and let the smells and sounds of summer evening cooking swirl around you in this cluttered shambled settlement, if you heard his voice

64

you'd know. There's some of old Archie's voice inside you somewhere.

I could hear him now as Jack and I walked from the car to the van. I followed him up the three steps to the rickety door. When Jack opened it up and called, 'We're here', the first thing I noticed was the smell.

Deb came out from the kitchen and a smell of a rich meat stew followed her. When she hugged me, a meaty cloud wrapped around me. Then she held me at arm's length and said, 'You look good, come in, come in.'

Inside, this van is small enough for you to reach up and push your hands against the thin roof. As soon as you walk in, the kitchen is there, to the left is the TV and chill room with a little table, so when you eat, you're sitting low on the sofa and this little table. On the right, there's a tiny corridor with three doors. One toilet and two little bedrooms. Now, we're standing in the kitchen, the three of us, filling it.

'Tell me then, how are you?' she said. Jack put my bag down and leaned against the worktop. Deb leaned back too and folded her arms. 'How are they treating you?'

'Good. It's fine. The doctors and everyone, the staff are all are nice.'

'What do you do during the days?'

'Um, we just, I just…'

Jack said, 'I'll put the kettle on. Are you hungry Amy?'

I told her a little about talks with the doctors, the garden we can go in, the room to play table tennis and board games.

'What do the doctors say?'

Deb was like a teacher, I thought of her then with her hair tied back and glasses, holding the book that I

65

never read and looking at me with this look that said, I know you don't know what you're talking about. You're wasting everybody's time and just adding to your own embarrassment, you didn't read the book, did you?

'They ask questions mostly. And we talk. I'm not sick really, not compared to the other people in there. It's more like I'm... um... tired all the time or something. It's all OK. I'm OK.'

'Amy, love, if it was all OK, if you were OK, they wouldn't be keeping you in.'

Jack reached across her to get three cups from the shelf. 'Alright, alright,' he said, 'if she says it's OK, then it's OK. I've got some of that cake you like Amy, reach behind you love and grab a few plates. Deb, can you see if your Mum is awake? Maybe she'll have tea.'

'I'm doing dinner, don't have cake yet.'

'How long is that going to be? Another hour?'

'Seventy-five minutes.'

'A little bit of cake then.'

The plates were stacked in the bottom shelf. When I turned around, the door was shutting, and Deb was gone. Jack was pouring water into the teapot. Without looking up he said, 'Sorry Amy, you know. She just wants to know if you're OK.'

'I know. I just don't know what to say.'

Out of the window I saw Debbie disappear into the opposite van. The cake was a sponge with cream and jam filling. This was the first time I'd held a knife in six months. When I pressed it to the sponge the cream squeezed out, then some of the jam seeped out too. I thought about a soft toy, something you'd cuddle in a cot then cut open for fun, just to see the inside, to see the stuffing, and then see that it was bleeding, really bleeding and you couldn't stop it because you'd cut the toy too

66

deep. Stupid, really stupid thing to think, I know, but there you have it. Deb came back in.

'She's asleep.'

'Can I see her?'

'No. It's best not. Later. Let's not disturb her now.'

* * *

After dinner I was tired. 'I'll have an early night if that's OK.'

'We all will. You're in the back bedroom. It's nice to have you back here where you belong, ' Deb said.

Jack said, 'If you need anything, just shout.'

The back room was small with a double bed and a window. My meds make me drowsy, so I climbed into the bed, but I couldn't sleep. I could hear them talking, not every word, but some disconnected sentences floated past me. I couldn't get comfortable. I heard Deb calling someone a thief. Jack's voice was low, I couldn't hear it properly, but whatever he said, Deb didn't agree with it. He needed a spine she said. Eventually I heard Deb leave, and the van went quiet, but I still couldn't get comfortable. The room had something in it, I was sure. Maybe it was a ghost getting ready. Gran's ghost then. But it wasn't. It wasn't so natural. It sounded like one of the generators, but it had a higher tone and a slippery tic. Slowly, I realised it was a machine. I opened my eyes and there it was, tucked in the corner by the door. There were two green lights blinking at the top and there was some kind of mechanism, a churning and quiet spitting, squeezing out little thoughts, long thoughts, used thoughts, new thoughts, heavy thoughts, broken thoughts, illuminative thoughts, bullet thoughts, perched thoughts, all piling up in the little space between the wall and the bed. I closed my eyes again and tried to rest. I wanted to be rid of my arms and legs. I couldn't find a place for them anywhere. I turned over and turned over, put my arms at my sides, pulled my legs at angles away, folded my arms under my breasts, stretched them above my head, straightened out my legs again, lay on my side, pulled my legs so my knees were near my chest and wrapped my arms around them, then stretched my arms and legs out wide, as far away from my body as I could, but no matter what I did, my limbs were in my way. Oh, just to get rid of them! I wished I was just a torso. Or at least that I could take away my limbs, or maybe that I could fold them away into my sleeping shape, like a bird.

Where I am valued, I belong. Where I am understood, I belong. Belonging is the comfort of others who stand not in judgement of me but in co–operative understanding with me. Belonging is the comfort of an environment which does not demand from me more than I can give. Belonging is where I understand the stories and my story is understood. Belonging is where I trust I am trusted. If the trust is violated, if my voice is supressed or if my story becomes misunderstood, though I may remain, I am now an outsider. I cannot belong where I am betrayed. Though I may be within, I no longer belong. The desire for belonging will drive me to find an other; the crueller the wound in me, the more extreme the denial of my voice, the more complete the exclusion of me, the stronger my reattachment to my newfound belonging.

Where I am valued, I belong. Where I am understood, I belong. Where my pain is acknowledged and legitimised, I belong. Now belonging is the comfort of a supported strength of position from which to vilify the other, that place where I was abandoned. Now belonging is the comfort of a co–operative understanding from which to justify myself and enrich my hostility to that which I do not belong. Now the comfort of a commonality of a targeted enemy nurtures a heated sense of belonging which binds all the more tightly. Now my story is not only understood, it is compressed, abridged and integrated. The tighter we bind together the more singular and simpler the narrative becomes. Now our belonging coheres and blunts our understandings of each lived experience. Now belonging is the comfort of not being the other. The exclusion involved, the denial, the sheer weight of it all, the longer we belong the simpler we become, the more us of there are together the blunter we become. We have not the flights of flocks of birds, we cannot make the swirl of a shoal, we have not telepathy or structural intelligence of the ant. Too many humans blunt each other. Stay sharp. Stay alone.

There was music coming from the kitchen. It was probably that beautiful serious dead singer. I got up and went through, and Jack was there, sitting on the worktop with his legs dangling, with a cup in his hands. The music had stopped. He'd turned the song off as soon as he'd heard me coming.

'Bad dreams?'

'No,' I said, 'I just can't sleep. I don't dream anyway. Or at least if I do, I can't remember. It's the medication. I usually just close my eyes and bam, next thing it's morning.'

'So, no sleep tonight?'

'Is it late?'

'Not too late.'

'Did Gran wake up?'

'Oh yeah. I washed her and she ate a little bit, but she's asleep again. I don't know if she knew I washed her, it's hard to tell what she knows now.' He sipped from his cup.

'Does she talk to you?'

'Sometimes. Mostly she's talking, thinking I'm someone else. Sometimes she's clear and she sees what's happening, she knows she's going. I don't know which is worse. It's so sad. She complains. Not all the time, I mean, sometimes she's lovely. It's just so itty bitty. It's all disconnected. She wanted to see the manager today. I had to tell her the manager was out, but I'd put in a formal complaint for her and he'd get it as soon as he came back.'

'How's Deb about it? And Mum?'

Jack sighed and sipped from his cup again before saying anything. He ran his hands through his hair and closed his eyes. It looked like there was something he really wanted to say, but he was stopping himself. 'As soon as this is done, I'm going to move away, further away this time. There'll be no reason for me to come back. Your Gran was so good to me. She's the only reason I'm here.'

There was a call from the other van. It was weak, but it said, 'Debbie, Debbie!'

Jack slid off the counter and out of the door. Through the window I saw Debbie go to the room in her dressing gown while Jack stood in the kitchen. The light from the windows spilled into the gap between the vans. Then Jack put his head out of the door and said, 'Amy come in, your Gran's awake.' I stepped across the threshold.

In the other van there was a different smell. It was a smell like the back of an old shop, one of the corner shops where the boiled sweets were kept in the big glass jars on the front counter. The back of the shop where the household things were kept, detergents and powders. It was a smell like that, like a washing powder poured over something old. I looked in from the doorway. The bed took up the whole room. There was just enough room on either side to stand, on one side a little chair was squeezed in and behind her headboard was a plastic window. The curtains were pulled, the light was on, the room was stuck in an odd twilight. She was sitting up, with pillows stacked around her. She looked so little, and her hair was a ball of white around her head. In school we had performances for the parents at Christmas and we'd have to dress up as Mary and Joseph or the shepherds. None of the costumes ever fitted anyone. Here was the smallest girl in the class dressing up as God. I inhaled deeper. Was it the sheets? Or her clothes? Or just her? Was this what the start of death smelled like? How long had she been dying? Right now, it was life stagnating, or in fact, reversing. Life becoming non–life. Maybe that was the smell. Non–life. Getting stronger.

She held out her arms as I got closer.

'Amy, my girl. Come here and kiss me.'

Jack and Debbie stood squashed in the little doorway. I leaned over the bed and kissed her cheek and hugged her. I was right. The smell was coming from her.

'Gran,' I said. 'How are you?'

'Oh, I'm feeling alright.' She raised her eyebrows and pursed her lips, making a silly face and looking at Jack and Debbie. 'If these two would let me get a moment's peace. They're ever so needy.' I laughed. Just a short little laugh but it was a laugh. Gran smiled at me

71

and squeezed my hand. It was weak little squeeze. Jack shook his head with a smile and Debbie dabbed her eyes with a tissue.

'No, Mum, just making sure you're alright.'

She made that silly face again and said, 'No, just making sure I'm still here. Well I'm not going anywhere.'

I sat on the chair next to the bed.

'Darling,' she said, 'how are you? Have they let you out?'

I looked up at Jack and Debbie. Jack looked surprised and Debbie nodded, so I said, 'Yes Gran, they have.'

'Are you better?'

'Yes Gran, I'm better.'

'You can sing again.'

'Um, no Gran. I'm not singing anymore.'

'Nonsense! Come on, sing something for me. I love your singing. Sing me a song.'

'Gran... I can't. I'm not singing.'

'Talk to me then.'

I didn't know what to say at first, so I started telling her about the hospital. I talked about the morning breakfast, the canteen, the plastic plants in the corridors, then Jack and Debbie left the room so I told her about the evenings spent sitting around the TV, while the other patients mumbled or sobbed or stared at the screen, or at the wall, scratched and smelled themselves, or tried to tell each other secrets about the world that only they knew but no one really listened because those weren't secrets for their worlds, not for the ones listening. There was no overlap, not really, and the inmates they were telling already had their own secrets about their own world they were telling themselves. I told her about the other girl in the room who had an episode, how she spent hours moaning and screaming in labour, trying to push out a baby that wasn't there, how she fought everyone off until she was put in isolation and was still trying to give birth. She's probably still in there now, trying to push out it out. I told her about the boy who, every morning, wants to go to the games room. Who flicks and tosses bits of cereal across the table at me with his eyes flashing and his smile spreading, but by the time the games room opens he's had his medication and is slumped on the couch drooling onto his chest, until the next morning when he wants to play again. She began to drop off, so I stopped and just watched her. Her skin was a dull yellowed colour. She looked like she was made of butter, but in this light I couldn't be sure. I went to stand up.

In the middle of the village was a tree. The tree had been there for as long as anyone had. Every day the people of the village sat in its shade and ate or talked and joked. There were berries in the spring and lush branches in the summer, and when the summer turned away there were nuts and the children collected them before school while they teased and played in the leaves around the wide trunk before the school master came and gathered them into the schoolhouse. Twice a year, the village held a feast and carnival in the centre of the village, and they put garlands and lights around the tree and the children made fabric herbal bundles to hang from the lower branches. Everyone knew that the tree was the soul of the village but no one had ever heard it speak until one day, the cobbler was smoking his pipe, watching the birds pick up lunch crumbs, and the tree said to him what it had to say and straight away he stopped his pipe and went straight to his wife who was cutting cabbages from the field. They went home together and made love. The village stayed the same through the years, the berries and the nuts, the nests and the falling leaves came and went, until one day a government survey man came. The tree, he said, would come down and in its place, there would be erected a statue of the leader. There were protests from the villagers and the gentleman said that the only compromise they would make would be to erect a pool and fountain at the base of the statue to wash the ruler's feet.

The cobbler's daughter was now a keeper of hawks and owls, and had a hawk which she'd trained from a nestling. She, and the rest of the village were furious at the plans, but sure enough, one day a team of men arrived to cut down the tree and lay the foundations for the statue. Of course, cutting the branches and trunk was very easy, but the ancient roots were more difficult. After a few days they carried concrete slabs and put a screen around the tree stump and the space around it. Behind this screen they continued to dig and dig, day after day. Now, the devil, who had not happened upon this village in a long time, the people being virtuous, passed one day and stopped to see what was going on. His interest was pricked when he saw the men carrying away bits of the tree and the heavy concrete, so he watched awhile. He sat beside the cobbler's daughter who too was watching the men carry away the tree and listening to them dig and pour concrete behind the screens. Once that is gone, I can come back, the devil said. You're a trickster, she said, you'll never be wanted here. Ah yes, he said but without the tree, there is nothing living for the village to gather around. That is perfect for me. There will be gaps between the people where I can get in. They watched for the rest of the day and finally, when the screens came down, the men digging and laying the base for the plinth had given up. There was no way for them to put the statue where they had intended, so they stopped and left. The soil was dug and overturned and there were concrete slabs and a concrete plinth where the statue would have gone, but they had decided to take the statue to the next town where it was easier to erect. I will stay, said the devil. I will fight you and tell the people about you, said the cobbler's daughter, you will not find it easy. The devil said, there's no way for a new tree to grow there now, without something growing there the people will listen to me and not you. But, I like you, so I'll make a deal. I will go away tonight and if you make something grow here, with just the air and the rain, I will stay away for as long as it grows. Once the life stops growing, I will come back and you will make my shoes. Then he left. The day got later and later and the night fell, and the cobbler's daughter stayed, looking at the huge stone plinth. The devil was right, nothing was going to grow there. She stayed all night thinking about the devil and his impossible trick, and then just as the sun began to rise, she went and stood herself on the plinth where the statue was going to go, where the tree once was. The devil came back and when he saw her upon the plinth, he laughed to himself. Now it was just a question of time. He would return every morning. When the villagers awoke, they saw what the cobbler's

75

daughter was doing. They brought her food, but she would not eat it. Her bird came and perched on her shoulder. At night they brought her blankets to wrap around herself, in the mornings the children played around her, teasing her and each other until the schoolmaster came and gathered them in. In the afternoon, the elderly came and ate their lunch and asked her if she would eat something, and when she refused, they said prayers for her and went back to gossiping. In the evening, teenagers met and flirted and the days passed like this. For weeks, the cobbler's daughter stood there, until she began to fall ill, winter was strong, and her strength began to go. Her hawk stayed on her shoulder, and the devil returned to take his opportunity as soon as she fell. One morning, as the children threw snowballs at one another, the bird flew and cobbler's daughter was about to fall. The school master, instead of gathering the children into the school room, stepped up and helped her down while he stood on the plinth. The children took her to the shop keeper who took her in and took care of her and all the while the schoolmaster stood there and grew colder, and the small winter birds came to him. The devil could do nothing, because the soul of the village was still alive and still growing, and the school master stayed there. When at last the school master grew weaker, the butcher then prepared to fast, and after him, the seamstress took the plinth until the cobbler's daughter was well enough to go back on, and she did. Since then, to this day there is always someone on the plinth, keeping the living village growing and the devil away.

I knew all of this in the time it took me to straighten up, and I understood it all and then I was standing and Gran was beneath me and I felt so tall, and I went to Jack and Debbie's van and told them that she was asleep.

'OK, I'll sort her out,' Jack said. 'I've got to say, that's the most lucid I've seen her in weeks Amy. It was like she was back again.'

Debbie hugged me. 'Oh Amy,' she said. They went back across. I stood at the door. Further down the field, past the crossing of washing lines, past the other vans, away from the light of the windows at the end of the row, I could see a tall white shape. I walked towards the owl. I walked until I could smell it. It smelt of old damp wood. It was taller than me by about a head and a half. Its feathers had a dull glow in the dark and there was such strength in it, when it shifted its feet again, shrugged its grey shoulders, moved its head back and forth, I wondered at its physicality, the sheer weight and power of it there in the night. I didn't step any closer, we just looked at each other from that distance. I was happy to see it. It shook its feathers and opened its beak, blinked, then was still again. I think it was happy to see me. We stayed like that for a while. I was getting wet. A light rain was falling. I turned and went back inside.

* * *

Jack was in the front room of the van putting a blanket on the sofa seat in front of the TV.

'Did I take your bed? I thought you were in the other bedroom.'

'I am, I just can't sleep at the moment,' he said, 'so I just doze in front of the TV, it helps me not think.'

'I know. I can't get tired.'

'Well I'm not tired yet either. Sit down. What do you want to watch?'

We sat together on the sofa. I tucked my legs underneath me and leaned on a cushion, and he flicked through the channels until we landed on a comedy we both liked. I'd seen it before. I think Jack had too, but we watched it for a while. Jack said, 'It must be tough, being in the hospital so long.'

I shrugged. 'You get used to it.'

'But you can't want to get used to it, right?'

The comedy was of two people sitting on a sofa too. The light rain was brushing against the shell of the van in soft waves. If I was back in the unit, I wouldn't even know it was raining. Here the membrane was so thin.

'I feel like I've been taken apart and put back together wrong.' I tapped my forehead. 'Not just this. My whole body. Inside too.'

'Well, look, we're all prisoners of our minds. All of us. I think the world is better with you in it, out here rather than stuck in there.'

'Yeah. That's what the doctors want.'

The programme ended. He passed me the remote. 'I don't mind now, you choose.'

I moved my feet out from under me and stretched my legs across the sofa, beneath the blanket, so my feet were touching his legs. I wiggled my toes. He smiled. I flicked around the channels. There was a show about ghost hunters. The picture was black and white, night vision, and there were people with cameras attached to their foreheads creeping around in the dark.

'How about ghosts Jack? Yes or no?'

'Yeah, I don't see why not.'

'Have you ever seen one?'

'No, but I think probably if you know there is then

there is. Like what you know before you learn. How about you?'

'I don't know. So when Gran goes, do you think she'll have a ghost?'

'Well, probably…' His eyes were still on the screen, watching a pale face talk to the camera. 'She already is the ghost. We all are, don't you think? It's hard to believe this is all we are. It's hard to believe that something like that, like you or me or Gran or him just stops. I dunno.'

'If everyone knew, if everyone knew there were ghosts then it would be a different thing.'

'Well it'd open up some opportunities, I think. But we can send these guys to find out. They're the experts.'

'Ha. They never really find them for sure.'

'No,' he said, 'never. But they're always still scared, check that out.' The people on the TV were getting more and more panicked, jumping at noises and grabbing each other. Their skin gave a transparent glow and their eyes were black with white dots in the middle, when they opened their mouths it was empty inside.

'Your Mum messaged me. Do you want to see her? She's going to call around tomorrow, but we could go out.'

'I don't know, I haven't seen her in so long. What does she say about me?'

'Well… she…'

'No, wait.'

'OK.'

'I don't want to know.'

'OK.'

We watched the rest of the TV show. The team didn't manage to get any footage, but they all felt a presence, they were all sure someone or something else was in the house with them. There were close ups of each of them. They all told the camera that they had not been alone in there. Close up, looking at the camera with that pale glowing skin and eerie black eyes, they looked like spirits, like they were the ones haunting the old house, ghosts as afraid of the dark as anyone. It ended, but not before they told us that next, they were going to visit the most haunted house in the country. Tales of decapitated ghosts, little children in the walls, voices that spoke at midnight, houses built on ancient burial grounds – all coming in the next episode. We wouldn't have had to wait if we'd wanted to watch it, because it started right away. I turned the volume down and I looked at Jack and he looked at me. There was so much more he wanted to say, I could see it, I could feel him reaching out to me in the silence. In that moment we both realised the rain had stopped. He squeezed my foot.

'How about a walk?'

* * *

The field was quiet. So many vans and trailers but so little noise. We walked down the rows. There were some pools of light and some bubbles of sound, some TV programmes, some conversations, some music, but each one was quiet, aware of itself, aware of how close it was to everything and how fragile their shells. In another step you were through the bubble and it was quiet again. Most of the vans were silent and dark, and there was just the low throbbing of the generators underneath it all, the chug chug chug of them webbed into a rhythm, the pulse of the night. As we walked, the owl flew high above around the edges, huge and utterly soundless. When I followed with my eyes, Jack looked at me and then to where my gaze led and followed it too.

'What'll you do when you come out? You could work on your music.'

'No, I can't do that anymore. I can't even listen to

music, it makes me so... songs do that, get inside, wake parts of you up. It was like that before I went in, but I kept trying, I kept singing. But Jack, the words just made me... I just got sadder and sadder. I really think that's what made me... whatever it was. Words make me sad.'

'When your Mum told me you'd been admitted, I've got to say, I actually thought, good. She'll get some treatment and some space. But it's been a while now, don't stay in there Amy.'

'I'll come out. When I'm better.'

I could tell that this wasn't good enough for him.

'How about you? When Gran goes?'

'I don't know, but I've got to get away from here. Debbie won't need me. Every time I do get away, I hit a boundary, or something pulls me back. It's like a magnet.'

'Speaking of boundaries.'

We came to the edge of the field. The path wound back on itself. We left the path and walked right around the edge by the fence. My feet were getting wet. It seemed like so long since my feet had gotten wet inside my shoes. I could feel my toes against each other, the fabric of my sock on my skin, I could sense the shape of the shoe more and more as it got wetter. A stupid little detail, but one that occupied me before I thought again of Jack and his magnet.

'You'd go into the city?'

'Further than that.'

'The city is grimy, don't you think? I thought it when you picked me up. Why does no one clean it? A good wash?'

'It rains enough.'

'No, it needs a power hose. Someone with a power hose.'

'Yeah it does. Maybe that's what I should do. Buy a power hose and clean the city.'

'I'll do it with you. I'll come out if we can clean the whole place.'

'Or at least just Gilden Street.'

We heard Old Archie's steel guitar before we came to the end of our row, and when we got to his van, Jack stopped for a moment to listen. I saw the owl had landed now, back to where it had been earlier, at the end of the row of vans, just in the shadow of the fence.

'Archie's got to be older than your Gran. By quite a bit.'

It was just a scratchy blues riff, over and over. A slight variation on the end of each phrase, but that was it. It sounded like he was humming along with it, but that could have been the pulsing drone of the generators.

'Well something's keeping him alive.'

We went back to the vans. I went straight to my cramped room and took off my shoes and clothes. I could hear Jack settling on the couch and the TV went on, some talking at a low volume, a shout, gunshots, theme music, ads. I leaned out the window and the owl was still there, tucked in by the hedge, legs folded away, sleeping. The thought machine churned in the corner. I lay down in the bed with my arms folded across my chest, like you would in a coffin. Neatly.

My boundaries extend as far as my voice can be heard and the resonance of my actions can be felt. If my voice is unheard or my actions unperceived then my boundaries cannot move, and I am held static by them. But when my voice is heard or my actions felt then I am the push, the shift, the movement. Boundaries are not barriers.

82

Boundaries do not keep people or ideas out. Boundaries overlap. The words of others that we quote and the actions of others we describe or repeat, these are boundaries overlapping, and when we use these words or repeat these actions, we are extending the personal boundaries of others. I cannot extend beyond my boundary, so when I encounter boundaries, inevitably they are my own. It is then my intent which can move them or not. My boundary is where I reach a point of choice. When I choose to act or use my voice, my boundary expands in that direction of intent, where my words are heard and my actions are felt, and at the edge of the expanding boundary I am that point, that moving point, the impossible balance upon the movement – that compressed concentration of all of my histories, of all of the stories that have made me, of all of the voices that are me, all of the actions that have brought me, that convergence of all of the momentum – teetering upon the thin swift sharpened blade of now. The extent of my boundaries is the result of a manifestation of my intent and its interaction with what is beyond the edge of me. As long as I use my voice and act with intent and will, my boundaries will always move.

I sat up in the bed and leaned over the edge. My hands searched around for a cable. I found the lead and then found the plug socket. I pulled out the plug. The thought machine's lights blinked once, it gave a big mechanic sigh and turned off.

* * *

I woke when I was covered in gentle light. I hadn't closed the curtains and the foggy daylight pressed against the window and the whistles and chirrups, the delicate sparks and bursts of sound, floated in the morning.

I went into the kitchen. The sofa was empty. I looked out the window. Jack and Deb were in the kitchen of Gran's van. He had his arm around her. Deb's eyes were so swollen and red, Jack looked so grey. I stepped into the morning air and looked down the row of vans. The owl was still there, its plumage glistening. It looked up at me with those clear orange eyes. It was just sitting, still, looking down the row of sleeping fragile nests, straight at me. I crossed over, went up the little steps and opened the door then stopped in the doorway. 'Has it happened?'

* * *

I went into the room. There she was, in the odd twilight, like she had been yesterday when I saw her sleeping. The smell was still there. There was a stillness that was new. They came and stood behind me.

'We just got up. The nurse is on her way.'

'The nurse? So she's—'

'Gone, Amy.'

We stood in the doorway until I said, 'Can I open the curtains?'

When I reached over the bed and opened them, I saw Gran in proper light for the first time since I had been back. I was right. She was made of butter. Dried butter. I sat in the chair. She was old. I could see it now, for the first time I could see the age of her. Life had always softened that number. Debbie went back into the kitchen and Jack stood in the doorway.

'Peaceful,' he said, before turning and following Debbie.

I didn't know what to say. In that moment, I wasn't thinking about Gran. I should have been, but I wasn't. I was thinking about me. How utterly selfish. I was thinking about the missing pieces of me. When I was put back together maybe some of me was missing. I was incomplete. Or maybe part of me was always somewhere else. Some people never join themselves up, so the other part is left wandering. Me. How much of me was here? I was the edges of me. Most of me was somewhere else. You don't have to be dead to have a ghost. If I went back to the unit, I wouldn't see the owl again. I wanted to. I didn't want to never see the owl again. So I started to sing softly. Oh the summer time is coming, the leaves are swiftly blooming... I wasn't sure when I started, about what would happen, but the words, I sent them out away from me, they didn't bother me this time, they weren't turning back into me, I was sending them out, so that they'd go into my Gran. I closed my eyes. That was it. To sing to someone, that was the secret, that was how I could do it again. Sing out of you, sing into someone. Sing to the outside. When you look hard enough beyond the cage, the bars disappear. And the wild mountain thyme grows around the blooming heather. Would you go lassie go... Words are not yours. Push them out, they don't belong to you, don't keep them to yourself, they'll make you sad, yes they'll make you sad, but the sadness doesn't belong to you either so don't try to own it, send that out too. Transform them, melody, melody, melody, and give the power to those words to move, to travel. A song will travel further than a scream. With my eyes closed, the room disappeared, and I saw the rest of it. In the other van, the blanket was still across the sofa, half on the floor, the thought machine stood silent, useless, Jack was walking slowly in the dull morning light with tears in his eyes, towards the tall owl. The tall white owl was standing up, spreading its enormous illuminative wings, wide enough to take us all in, shaking them, throwing light into the morning and stretching its neck and tilting its head and looking at him approach in that weird owl way, the orange and black eyes seeing everything that was, all of our ghosts, all of the parts of us we were looking for. Debbie was standing on the van steps looking at Jack walking to the end of the row, her mouth agape and her body frozen, but for the thin shaking of her crumpled tissue and the trembling wonder in her eyes. And we'll all go together to pick wild mountain thyme…

From far off, I heard the van door open, footsteps coming up behind me, and the smell of each morning's miracle getting closer and closer and then suddenly, Jack's voice broke into me, a hammer breaking a shell, 'Oh my God!' then a shout, 'Deb! Dear God! She's alive again! Deb! Deb! She's alive again!'

INVASION

'Sweet Jesus… look at that.'

'This is crazy.'

They rolled to a dusty stop on the ridge. Alan and Manu leaned forward towards the windscreen to look at the beach below. It was red. A blood red block had been dropped and shattered. Right down to the waves was fractured movement and the tiny broken pieces were alive, teeming with freedom.

'In some cultures, they eat them. Roasted.'

'Alan. Come on. The only reason they eat them is because there's nothing left once they've been. They eat everything. Crazy. Look at that.'

'Millions.'

'Millions and millions.'

'Can you see this Jed?'

'Hang on. Where are the wipes? He's dripping.'

Alan turned awkwardly in the small car and reached into the back to wipe Jed's chin.

'He can't see from there.'

'Ah, he's got to see this.'

Manu pushed his nose and the tips of his fingers against the windscreen.

'Seriously. Sweet Jesus. They're still landing. We've got to go down. Get him out.'

'Will we be able to get the chair down d'you think?'

Alan twisted round again, opened the door and stepped out of the car.

'They're everywhere.'

He was standing in the middle of the frenetic criss-cross of locusts. Glinting metallic red bodies and black wings trembled around him like the projection of a film being played too fast. Someone was flicking the pages of the world's longest book. Little bodies, like sniper lights, rushed and buzzed and thudded against him, dropped, buzzed again and flew away. He laughed and walked to the edge. There was a steep incline. A muddy path, like a wound, ran down between the rocks.

'Yeah. We'll get him down. C'mon. Let's get him out.'

'C'mon Jed. You've got to see this.'

* * *

They had started to arrive during the night, when the wind had changed direction. A new wind, a fast wind, came hard to the island. It was supposed to bring rain. By morning there was a scattering of locusts in the town. People were noticing them sitting in the bushes and chewing through the flower stalks. As Manu and Alan drove to the hospital, more were appearing in the sky. By the time they wheeled Jed out, everything green was blotched red, and the sharp morning sunlight changed to a glow filtering through thin clouds of crimson.

* * *

When they got Jed out of the car and into the chair they were sweating.

'You've put on weight my man. Grab his hat.'

'He's lost it for sure.'

'Grab his hat.'

Alan pulled the hat and another pack of wipes from

the foot well. He fitted it on Jed, and wiped away the ones that were landing on the brim.

'Are they biting?'

'No. Not me anyway. This is going to be fun, getting down.'

The path was steep and uneven. The rocks poked through the sand and halfway down the slope the carpet of moving, shuffling, burying red backs began. Alan started to push the chair along the path toward the edge, but within a few metres the wheels were sinking into the sand.

'I don't know.'

'What d'ya think Jed?'

Alan crouched and wiped locusts from Jed's lap.

'Will we get you down to the beach to see this crazy thing? Will we carry you down? Or carry the chair? Will we? D'you want to see this? D'you want to see this crazy thing?'

Manu stepped next to him and handed him the wipes. Alan wiped Jed's chin again, then stood up and scanned for an easier route. More and more were landing. Manu grunted.

'It'll be like training. We can do it. I've carried that big lump in Telic. Right? Just imagine Gunner shouting the order. We can do it.'

'Well, Manu, that's digging deep.'

'Yeah. Well. A long time ago.'

'Do you remember his thing, his rant about the Dutch Afrikaans and their Mauser rifles?'

'Gunner?'

'Yeah. The Dutch Commandos kept using narrow gauge Mausers while the Brits kept trying to get bigger and bigger bullets. The Brits were trying to get a higher kill ratio but the Dutch kept using the Mauser, which was less likely to kill.'

'That was nice of them.'

'It took two, sometimes up to three people to look after the injured soldier. By injuring, not killing, one, you disable at least three. Three disabled soldiers instead of one dead one. Drain the enemy's resources. You've still got to feed them if they're alive. Still eating but not fighting.'

'Huh. Again. A long time ago man, a long time ago.'

'It's not. It's not that long ago.'

* * *

Alan and Manu stood and watched for a while, facing the fast wind. They didn't flinch now when the buzzing bodies flew into them. The volume and speed of the insects, the way the swarm broke the light into snaps and tangled the sound of the sea was mesmeric. They were inside a rattling and swirling, a noise of stones being shaken in a bowl. The only steady rhythm was the sea washing in and dragging out the edge of the glistening bubbling blanket of beach. Dark wet sand was clean, for just a second, and then bled again. All along the coast, they were the only ones. Theirs was the only car to roll along the bumpy dirt track, around the base of the old volcano, the stony fields and broken wooden stiles. and time buckled fruit trees now stripped of their green and standing bare and bloodshot, leaving the roaming goats to chew on the sticks.

Manu turned and walked along the ridge to scan for an easier route. Alan crouched next to Jed again, wiped his lap and rubbed the back of his hand.

'Manu's on recce. He'll come back with a route. Have you ever seen anything like it? We'll get you down Jed, we'll get you down.'

* * *

But when Manu came back, he was shaking his head.

'I don't know.'

'No?'

'Well, there's getting down, and then there's getting back up.'

'There's leaving the chair. Can we leave the chair?'

Manu walked to the edge of the path again. The buzzing red cloud was getting lower now. The swarm was draining from the sky and settling on the beach. He looked back inland.

'Jesus, they've devoured everything. There wasn't much to start with but now, look, there's not even a flower left. I don't know man. It won't be comfortable for him, for us to carry him down.'

'No. But–'

'And just one slip.'

'Yeah, it's too much.'

'Well one of us should. Go down. Look at it.'

'You go. Take point.'

'OK. I'll go.'

Manu disappeared over the edge. Alan crouched down again.

'Jed. Jed. Where have they come from? How far? D'you think they wanted to come here? Jed? What d'you think?'

He wiped Jed's chin again and looked into his eyes, trying to put himself in there.

* * *

He unzipped the bag and took out a Tupperware box. A drop of rain fell on the lid, then another. A shadow passed over them. Alan saw more shadows approaching on the sea, far in the distance.

'Here it comes then.'

He rooted around to find a spoon. When he got one, he settled next to the chair and prised the lid off.

'This is mud.'

He spooned some out and held it to Jed's lips, pushing just a little bit.

'There's a way to stop them you know. I read about it. There's a parasite that, if it gets in their guts, stops them from swarming. It messes with their pheromones, communication systems. They can't send each other messages. Get them to eat it. A parasite on the inside. That can stop them.'

Now Jed's eyes were drifting, one eyelid half closed, his drooped lips opened then he slowly swallowed. The pits in his cheeks sucked in, and he took a breath. Locusts crawled on his hat, dropping from the brim and buzzing away. Alan got another spoonful and lifted it to his lips. Jed ate.

'Jed, what's in this mud? And there's another thing. I read it too. About feasts. In Africa with the tribes. They divided up the food at feasts. There were rules. About how it was divided up, you know? So, elderly men were given the tongue and the right haunch, married women were given the fat and the breastbone. Beggars were given the ass and balls or whatever, and the leaders ate the liver and the kidneys. But the warriors, the warriors, listen Jed, the warriors had this – meat from the head, hooves, guts and tail all stuffed in the stomach and boiled. There was more for the other people, like the children, and the adolescents, they had the brains, I think. But that's what I remember. The warriors. Head, hooves, guts and tail.'

* * *

Below, Manu reappeared in sharp relief against the broken living red beach. He had taken off his shirt. He was walking toward the rocks on the edge.

'He's going for the rocks. Oh, Jed, man, we should have a photo. What d'you think? Photo op?'

Alan put the food back in the box and stood, taking his phone from his pocket. He wiped around Jed's chin again and brushed off the locusts that were crawling around his collar and up his neck and the ones that were landing on his lap and the brim of his hat. He turned the chair around so that the beach was behind and stood back. The red mist had dropped right down now, and pooled over the beach. Over the sea, clouds were coming in quickly. In the centre of the frame, Jed sat, hat drooping and head lolling, his arms limp, one palm facing upwards, the other wrist twisted uselessly in his lap and his legs angled as if letting someone pass. His mouth stretched, pulled on by an invisible hook. His eyes strained against the tilt of his head, trying desperately to see who had caught him, and just beyond his range of sight someone was reeling him in. Alan's finger hovered over the button, then he lowered his phone.

Below, Manu had reached the speckled rocks on one side of the beach. The clouds were racing in now, riding the wind, the dark shapes on the sea bringing a fast approaching line of battle and Alan tasted the rain in the air. Manu was standing on the rocks tall and still, solid and muscular, waiting for the order.

Alan stepped to the edge. Then it happened. The rain shadows hit the shore. Manu jumped from the rocks onto the beach and started to run. He ran in a straight line across the strand. The locusts burst up all around him in a frantic clicking and buzzing cloud, rippling rich colour back into the sky. The thin rain was falling now

93

and the swarm started to glisten into millions of tiny reflections of light. Rising up from the running shadow on the shore, the shimmering red wave pushed up from the beach to the ridge, advancing fast, and before Alan could take a breath, his body was blasted with the buzzing thudding insects. The noise was so loud now, like radio interference, and Alan couldn't tell if the glittering locusts were moving up or down, like confetti on a victory parade. He tried to see the beach, to see Manu, but it was all out of focus, so he submitted. He closed his eyes and lifted his chin and listened to the thousands of tiny attacks on his body and his skin, concentrated on each little thud, felt carefully each time he was hit and felt on his face the soft shroud of rain that would soon cover everything.

Then. Behind him. Breaking through, he heard something like a voice, urgent, distorting, strangling, panicked... 'Wait out!'

With his back to the beach, Jed was rocking and straining. Alan grabbed the chair and turned him. Jed was covered in locusts; they had swarmed him. His head was tilted back, and they were on his face, moving over his eyes, two were crawling into his open mouth as he was shaking, shouting these words as twisted sounds, struggling against a second death.

'Wait out! Wait out! Wait out! Wait out!'

CUT

Day 1

Boxes ticked on prep; nice one CJ and Andy.

All shots covered.

Check 3rd frame 05 and 06 – birds taking off from river, landing on the field behind – POTENTIAL FOR OPENING/ESTABLISHING SHOT.

Simon and Abby have some tension, it wasn't there in readings. Interesting takes.

Think about close ups, for 12/13/14 – Thursday.

Forecast is overcast – check Happy Pilgrim back room in the morning for alternative scene 3.

Sort shopping list – plants/plastic plants at least 1.5m, also STOCK FOR CATERING.

Day 2
Yes on close ups of Simon, not for Abby.
05/06. ✓

Forecast good, maybe catch sundown over the Bodach Drum if timing is right. The ridge is stunning, steep and wild, great for the last shot. Location looks amazing, the dawn rain is good as it means everything is vibrant and wild looking.

Amend 13, less script; NO NEED NO EXPOSITORY OR 'THERE'S ALWAYS SOLITUDE…' DIALOGUE.

I have doubts if we even need the V/O. Simon carries it in the scene.

Happy Pilgrim is great – landlord CALLAN. Perfect location. Drum is short few mins drive away.

Catering – needs delivery before 11:00. It is pretty isolated here, but they knew that in the contract.

Day 3

Jesus, Simon can be harsh. What the hell happened? Abby was a mess by 5:00pm. Need to have a word with both first thing. Maybe a rehearsal?

Catering a mess. Rethink this.

Tight close on Simon, yes, working a treat. Drop the V/O? Find out in post, I guess.

Tomorrow use jib shot for 17. Forecast is poor, overcast, occasional rain all day.

Winter is here. The Pilgrim is a great shelter for us.

Day 4

Changed catering to the Pilgrim. Callan = legend

Coming together piece by piece. Simon is carrying this. A great principal, he has the strength.

For wide on 19 – use sync. ✓

Combined 20/22 into single for change of location to the Pilgrim. Tungsten. Gel 3A ✓

Cloud was too low on the hill for EXT closing shot. Next time.

The extra time spent on reveal scene 20 was worth it. Long takes two shots – electric. Glad we didn't do the rehearsal now. Abby was uncomfortable, don't think she was acting. Nothing like the read through, much better. WOW.

Don't use 2nd C for long scene T3 light changes in later takes.

09, 14, 15 revise and schedule reshoot. Will we have time on the last day with Abby?

Call Martyn about the editing schedule – call Gina re budget.

Check Adam and CJ's PD transfer. They've been great. Ask CJ about next year's project.

Forecast favourable for final shot over the hill tomorrow sunset.

Day 5

More rain, so location in Pilgrim until 14:30, then it cleared, but still no closing shot, though the rain was on and off, the cloud cover was too heavy for the light. The whole point of this location was the sunset this time of year, when everything turns to gold. Our hero needs to walk over the hill.

Simon did the long walk three times up the Drum but we can't use any of it. It's steep. He's not young. He must have been tired. Can we get drone? ASK ANDY re DRONE.

Try again tomorrow. Forecast is good.

Check 26. Abby's last shoot tomorrow – REMEMBER TO PICK SOMETHING UP. Wine and flowers? CJ says red. Think she'll be glad to go.

Yes, no need for V/O, Simon says it all in his eyes. A wasted day on that. Still, it'd always there if we decide we need it in post.

Tomorrow reshoots 09A (tracking), 09B, 14 (develop from Simon to Abby) run into 15 without 'a sanguine sorrow' line – though it is one of Simon's favourites. Too much dialogue.

Simon's got a room upstairs in Pilgrim. Handy.

Day 6

Got a room upstairs in Pilgrim. Nice, small, warm. Window to Bodach Drum – looked beautiful this morning. No rain. Evening was good light, but plenty of kids and parents climbing up the hill for a random school or flag festival or something, lots of cars and flags, still no final shot. DO WE REALLY NEED THE FINAL SHOT?

Reshoots complete✓ …the 'sanguine sorrow' remains, Simon wouldn't let it go.

Final two shot complete ✓

Abby gone. She's done well under the circumstances. Don't think she liked it up here, a bit remote for her.

News from Gina that the release budget has been reduced to nothing – this might not even get out anyway.

35 check C1, T4 and 5 BACKGROUND ACTION. No PB's tomorrow…

Day 7

Rain, low cloud. But good day.

No filming, just time in the Pilgrim. Forecast is good, we can get it all tomorrow. Turned into a long drinking day. CJ and Andy are good for next year's Brigand project. Already some ideas coming out.

Spoke to Simon about the final shot. Hahahaha. Yes we need the shot, yes, are you crazy, it's not just me disappearing over the hill, it's me getting over the arc of this affair, it's my immersion into the landscape I've been working on, it's me re-joining and renewing the real relationship with the real love of my life, the land. He got VERY fiery. Well it was a long day and at some point, we all did about different things. CJ turned to politics again. When you're in the Pilgrim all day not shooting but drinking there's going to be something at some point. Good laugh though. All in all, a good day. I left at 21:40.

Forecast for tomorrow is good. 36, 37, 38 and last dialogue and a LOW LIGHT SINGLE for 26 (C1 tight on Simon with Bodach Drum IV, then pull to focus) – all tomorrow. I think. I feel like it's 3:00 in the morning. It's only 22:15. We're coming to the end anyway. WE'LL ALL BE HOME SOON.

Day 8

Receipts and expenses PD checked.

All other shots are done except the final. The pieces have come together. Editing will be tight, but I know what to do.

YES ON 3 FRAME 06 for OPENING SHOT with birds ✓ I knew it, it's gorgeous.

Gina is not hopeful about funding. She's in a panic.

Should be finished, but Simon wants to stay on until we get the final shot. I told him he doesn't have to, that we've got some great establishing shots, landscape, some silhouettes etc, but it's important to him. And he's right. It's an important shot, it will complete the emotional narrative of the whole thing. So, I've asked Adam and CJ to stay another day to get it. I feel like it's Simon's story in a way. I know he feels like that.

We will get the shot tomorrow.

Day 9

Bloody hell. I think we got it. Morning of rushes and shooting in the pm. Got some close-ups and a drone thanks to Adam before the long walk. We got it, but Simon didn't. It looks good, close up tight face shot starting up the hill, pull back, then reverse angle over the top of the ridge. He wasn't happy with the way he disappeared. We had it in the bag at T3, but he wanted to do it AGAIN, so we just shot till the light was gone. The winter hill looked amazing. Illuminative. Adam and CJ gone home. They left straight after the shoot. Worn thin, I think. A long drive through the night for them.

In the Pilgrim for drinks with Simon and he says he wants to spend TOMORROW LOOKING FOR THE RIGHT SHOT. Whaaaat? Maybe we'd been thinking about this wrong. Why sunset? The place, of course, but there's no reason narratively for it to be sunset. Talked about it. In the end I had to agree. Bastard. Hahahaha. So, we're doing it again tomorrow. OK. I can last here another day and Simon – SO passionate about this and maybe he's right. This place is amazing. There's a magic all day, and let's try and catch all of it.

Day 10

Oh my God.

Start off, Simon woke me at 5:30, I was still drunk, I think. The shot at sunrise, maybe that was it. Cold, cold. Started in near darkness, single tight light on face walking up the hill. Ghostly. Full of shadows. A face in the shadows, eyes fixed on the top of the Drum. Again and again. How many times did he want to walk over this hill? Back at 10, ate Pilgrim breakfast Callan lit an early fire for us, then back outside. Simon looks ragged in shot A and even more in closeup. In the pm he was stumbling over the top. We had a long talk. I wanted to stop. He wanted to use the day, while it was still here, and we were still here. How many more times? Oh my God, kept shooting till light went and his face was a ghost again. Back to the Pilgrim. I'm exhausted. That's it. Done. A whole day on the slope of Bodach Drum. I could make the whole film just him going over the horizon line now.

HOME TOMORROW!

It's 3:00 am. Noise in the hall woke me, heard the key in the door. Opened the curtain just in time to see Simon walk away. In costume. Is he drunk? Drinking in his room? He's not walking drunk. Dammit. I'll have to check.

Just back in. COLD COLD COLD. Jesus. Simon's not drunk, he's gone to the hill. I tried to drag him back. Its 3:55. Sleep and home tomorrow.

Day 11

Left at 9:40. Simon not in his room or answering his phone, Callan saw him at breakfast looking rough but not since, so stopped at Bodach Drum. Saw him appear over the ridge, walk down to the spot and turn around and go back up. I walked up the Drum to him, there's no need WE HAVE THE FUCKING SHOT but when he came back down, he wouldn't talk, just turned around in character and went back up.

Home 17:00.

Rushes check. 14, 15. COMBINE 1&2. Review closing shot. I'll have to find time; it's going to take a while. SO MANY takes.

Gina's worried about the distribution contract – funding is evaporating, BUT she's got another lead. Gina's great. Talk am, reschedule post prod? YES. Maybe best, I need a break for a few days.

He's still not answering his phone. Called Callan. Simon was in for his dinner, then straight back out again still in costume. If he does it enough times he'll disappear over the hill and never come back.

Yes, reschedule post prod. I need to rest.

SILK

The banging from the trunk stopped. Now George could just hear road noise, the steady drone on the quiet night road. There was nothing to interrupt the momentum of his headlights cutting through the darkness. Not a single car passed him. His shirt was damp with sweat. He rolled down the window and took some deep breaths, exhaling slowly. His grip on the steering wheel relaxed and then his foot relaxed off the accelerator, and he began to feel back in control. Now he could think.

There was no major town between him and the long sandy beach. He knew this road well, every bend and dip, and could visualise each lay-by and country lane from here to the open sea. He had just passed Reynold and was approaching Stockbridge. Then, he would follow the winding road to the sleepy village of Ashton Peak, and beyond, to the flat farmland before the steep turn down to the coast. The clouds were clearing and the half-moon moved smoothly across the sky like his headlights across the land.

What was he going to do with Jonny? The white anger rushed in again, filled him. Dammit anyway. He slammed his hand on the steering wheel. Jonny had brought this on himself. Dammit. The banging from the trunk started again, but without the moans of before, just thudding, and then stopped abruptly. He'd calm down in a few miles. He was probably sobbing to himself in the small darkness of the trunk. Good. Let him cry. What was he thinking, going to his house again? George was on his way home, just a few streets away, when he saw him. He pulled over and got out and Jonny walked up to him and started shouting something. As he got closer, George saw he was swaying and his eyes were unhinged, looking in different directions. He was drunk. His thin voice rang around the neighbourhood, but his words were distorted. It sounded like, 'She wears silk! If she knew you! If she knew you! I'd be in silk!'

George tried to talk with him, to hold him steady, but Jonny spat at him and started to slap and claw, so George grabbed him and tried to hold him harder, but Jonny was thrashing, so George opened the passenger door of the car and pushed him in. When he got in the other side, Jonny launched himself at him. He turned in the seat, climbed on him, squeezing past the steering wheel, scratching and spitting words about silk. George tried to push him back, he could smell the thick whiskey on his breath and the cramped space filled with frantic muffled moans, clenched teeth and limbs, thrashing against the window and seats. George got the door open and pushed, and Jonny tumbled out onto the road. Then he scrambled to his feet and started to run towards the house. Now there was nothing else but the sweat and rage of the moment, and in a second, George was behind him. He grabbed Jonny by the arm, spun him around and slapped him hard across the face, twice, first with his open palm and then with the back of his hand. Even though Jonny was smaller than him, he didn't fall. His head snapped to the side and some blood dripped from his mouth. There was a second of stillness. Then George pulled him and opened the passenger door of the car, but Jonny started struggling and shouting again, so he dragged him to the back of the car, pressed the lock and the trunk sprang open. He grabbed his torso and his legs, and with one heave, threw him in. He slammed the trunk shut on Jonny's screams, got in the driver's seat and sped away.

* * *

He should have seen something like this coming. He knew Jonny was crazy when he handed in his first assignment. It was a rambling free verse tale of a little girl lost in the woods who was found by a woodcutter. The woodcutter took the little girl back to his cabin and made her his wife. There they remained, and knowing nothing else, she began to love her forested isolation. She gave names to all of the trees and flowers that she saw growing around her, but as she grew it became clear that he had damaged her so badly she would never bear children. Her sorrow was such that she would not talk or eat or let anything pass her lips and so the woodcutter set about carving children from the trees in the wood which she looked after like a real family, and with her family of wooden children she at last began to believe that she had real happiness.

Jonny had a gaunt and fractured look about him, but when they locked eyes, George found it difficult to pull away. Right from the start, George viewed him with an uneasy combination of revulsion and lust. His eyes were always circled with eyeliner, sometimes he wore a pale lipstick and sometimes his lips were red. He dressed in thin t-shirts, tied up at the front showing his smooth flat stomach, the perfect little dent of his navel. He wore ripped denim jeans and bandanas in his unkempt hair. George purposefully kept this scruffy, thin, effeminate teenager at arm's length, but when they made eye contact, Jonny may as well have been grinding against him.

The writing assignments became more sexual and even more bizarre. One described the physical sensation of a virgin's orgasm induced by the voice of a preacher delivering a fiery sermon. Another was a long poem in rhyming couplets about a pig farmer's wife who loved her animals, especially the big old boar. The wife would not give herself to the farmer and so he forced her to sleep in the sty and eat from the trough. Soon she gave birth to a litter of twelve tiny children with pig's heads and trotters for feet. The farmer fattened and killed them all.

In lectures, he always sat at the back and George tried his best not to catch his gaze, concentrating on his other students, even feeling relief when he didn't attend. George was thinking about him more and more. There was a terrible tension that needed to be resolved. Thinking of him created this conflict inside, a chemical reaction, filling his stomach with fire and freezing his spine, muddying his brain. Even when lying in bed next to Alice, as she went through the plans for their thirtieth anniversary party, who to invite and what to have on the buffet, he was seeing Jonny's thin lipsticked mouth. He knew it was only a matter of time.

Within five weeks of him reading the story about the children of wood, they were drunk in a grubby hotel room at two in the afternoon in a frenzy to get each other undressed. Jonny started to squeeze and slap George's chubby chest and pull at his grey wiry chest hair, and George grabbed his wrists hard and said, 'Don't you mark me.' Jonny struggled then and George pinned him to the bed. Jonny's skin was so clear, smooth and

110

stretched tight over his frame, George was mesmerised. This body, this thin perfect unblemished body he was pinning to the bed and pushing his crotch against, was so like him when he was young, so long ago. That sudden remembering in that moment was like remembering a different person completely. A different person with so much future. Jonny wrapped his legs around George's waist and pulled him down, kissing him, opening his mouth wide, and George thought, my God he wants to swallow me, and Jonny hissed into his ear, 'I bet you hate me.' George had never felt anything like it before. The lust exploded inside him, the heat spread like a bomb blast through his body and there was a white blindness as they writhed together in a hysteria, with Jonny crying out obscenities and George commanding him to shut up, a mess of shrieks and thudding and shouts and moans, before at last they lay side by side taking in great gulps of musky charged air.

Jonny said, 'I respect your relationship with your wife.'

George said, 'Don't you ever fucking mention my wife again.'

* * *

There was a small narrow road, typically used by farm vehicles, just after Ashton Peak. It led to a clearing up on the brow of the dale and there began a wood which stretched down to the coast. It was a peaceful spot. He could see it now, miles from any houses, quiet in the moonlight. That seemed like the place to do it, to take him out of the trunk.

The clock on the dashboard said 00:43. Alice would be asleep. She wasn't expecting him home tonight. He was going to surprise her, coming home a night early from the conference. Again, anger swelled within him and he gripped and slapped the steering wheel. Had he not decided to come home early, what would have happened? He imagined Jonny and his wife on the doorstep of his house; Jonny in his cut-off denim shorts, ruffled hair, and dirty mascara tears, and Alice in her nightgown, torn between shutting the door on this crazy teenager and taking him inside and telling him to calm down, calm down.

George concentrated hard. He thought about what he'd say to him when he opened the trunk. One approach was to threaten him; to tell him if he ever found he was trying to contact Alice again, he would finish what he had started and bury him where no one would ever find him. Or he could be gentle and apologise. He was sorry; he could hold him close and talk softly, he could tell him that despite himself he had fallen in love with him and was working on a way for them to be together. Both of these were lies. He could not imagine himself killing Jonny any more than he could imagine being in a relationship with him; eating dinner with him, waking up in the morning with him, introducing him to friends, ringing him to say he was running late but was there anything he wanted from the shop on way home. The idea of it was ridiculous. In fact it was easier to visualise his hands around his neck, squeezing too hard.

* * *

Jonny's attendance at Uni had dropped off. He hardly came to class, he just called to the office to arrange when and where they were going to meet. It was wherever George could find that was the cheapest room with the earliest check in time. The first time Jonny said,

'Wouldn't it be nice to have a place, just for us, somewhere we could make our own, just you and me', he agreed and kissed him and said yes, that would be wonderful. Now, when Jonny said that, he remained silent, and the words just stayed there, floating, uncomfortable in the space above whichever bed they were in. That wasn't the only thing he suggested. Once Jonny said, as soon as they got through the door and George started to grab him, 'I need something else to wear for you. Won't you buy me something? Wouldn't I look good in silk?'

That was after he'd handed another assignment in. A story about a child, a girl with no eyes, whose experience of the dark world was just through her touch and taste and the sound of her brother's voice. Her favourite place was the rocking chair, her favourite taste was cinnamon-dusted soft bread and her favourite touch was silk. She listened to this voice, the voice that said it was his hand that was leading her, the voice that told her what the world was, who she was, and what it was she was touching and tasting.

It was six weeks after the first hotel room, and they were getting drunk in the upstairs room of The Dockers Bar. He asked Jonny if he was always attracted to much older men, to which Jonny replied, 'How about you and younger men? I don't believe you that you've never gone with a man before.' He took George's hand and pulled it to his crotch. 'You like it too much to have never wanted one before. It's not a switch that suddenly turns on.' George took his hand back and picked up his drink. The beer tasted gritty and smoky. Jonny looked at him and pursed his lips. 'But I knew there was something in you when I saw you. Something that didn't fit.'

Jonny was drinking double tequilas and George was

drinking glasses of dark beer and shots of bourbon. Besides them, there were only three other drinkers in the bar. Old men sitting by themselves, faces blotched and rugged, stinking and silent. There was only twenty minutes before the check in for the hotel next door. When George had asked what had made him come all the way down here from London he replied, 'London is a dangerous place.' Now George didn't ask him any more about his past. After all this time, George really didn't want to get to know him at all. And when he spoke about himself, about his tragedy of a childhood, his moving from family to family, his misadventures and his medications, George didn't know how much to believe anyway. Jonny rambled and wove his stories much like the way he wrote. George didn't want him to start talking about his past, or to start asking for things, or saying, 'Wouldn't it be nice if…'

So he said, 'Your stories, you know, your stories are fantastic.'

Jonny said, 'Why don't you give me better grades then?' His skinny hand moved on to George's thigh, moving upwards.

'Because,' George replied, 'your punctuation and grammar and formatting are terrible. I said your stories were fantastic, not your writing. There are rules you must follow if you want to get the higher grades.'

Jonny took his hand off George's leg and picked up his glass again.

'I don't care about rules or grades or achieving. That's your side of things. That's academia. That's all suits and pleases and thankyous.'

'You have such a dark twist to what you do, your stories. I'm surprised you haven't worked the devil into one of them.'

'The devil!' Jonny screeched and laughed. 'What an old-fashioned idea! Who is the devil? There's no need for the devil! Why deal with the devil when you have a world of damaged people right in front of you?'

* * *

George took a sharp left turn off the main road. He hadn't passed a single car. He knew for certain that this quiet farm road would be deserted. He needed time and space to talk with him. He needed to find out why Jonny had gone back to the house. He needed to find a way to make Jonny see that going to Alice wouldn't solve anything for anyone, to make him see that when you're young you just want to be understood but when you're old you learn it's better if people don't fully understand you. As he approached the brow of the hill, he resolved that he would promise Jonny anything he wanted as long as he didn't try to contact Alice again.

Already, he was thinking what he would say to Alice; 'I've got this crazy student…' He'd paint Jonny as a fantasist with a crush who had made passes, and when George told him that there was no way anything would happen, he'd gone off the handle and vowed to destroy his life. He was sure Alice would go for it. She'd seen Jonny once before, when he called to the house while George was at work. Alice was alone, working, when the bell rang, and she opened the door to what she described as a young man dressed up like a teenage girl. George was sitting opposite her, eating, when she told him. He felt all of his blood drain from his skin, his brain emptied, he felt dizzy. He kept his head down. Alice kept talking. 'He said he was a gardener and was looking after people's gardens in the estate.'

'A gardener?'

'Yeah. He knew all of the plants and flowers we have at the front, the names, and their seasons, when they came into bloom. He said he'd come by once every few weeks, weed and prune and the like. He seemed quite nice. A bit strange, but nice. Smiley. It has got in a mess, the front, I haven't looked at it for the longest time, and the fence at the back.'

George could hardly swallow. He didn't want to. Alice would see how difficult it was for him. He got up to get a glass of water. From the sink he said, 'Are you going to get him in?'

'No, no. I thought about it, but no. We can do it ourselves.'

He sat down again. 'Good, we've enough going out at the moment.' The conversation changed but his blood didn't return for the rest of the night. When he'd confronted Jonny with this, Jonny was sitting on a bed in another rented room, unbuckling his belt and he was standing over him unbuttoning his shirt. Jonny squirmed and looked away and said, 'Well, I do gardening. It's one thing I know about, how things grow, how to look after them. What do you think I do? How was I to know it was your house?'

He wanted to threaten him then, but didn't know what to say. If Jonny went to the house again, then he'd do what? He couldn't take his eyes off him. This beautiful boy. There was an anger inside him, but all he could think was, oh how I wish I had red lips.

* * *

He pulled up onto the grass clearing off the road and stopped the engine. The night was still, the sky clear, the half-moon bright. He was much calmer now than he was twenty minutes ago. He was seeing a way past this situation now. Alice would believe him. There was no way she'd think that he'd want to mess with a boy like that. This could all be handled. He just had to calm Jonny down.

He felt confident and in control and he knew exactly what he was going to do.

What he didn't know was that when he had struck Jonny his brain had rattled inside his skull. The blood vessels and membranes his medications were protecting were bruised, and when George threw him into the trunk, his head had collided with the wheel arch. By the time he drove away from the streets of his home, Jonny's brain was bleeding. As Jonny screamed and writhed and beat his hands against the trunk, a heaviness and dizziness was taking over him. On the winding road through Reynold, he was drifting in and out of consciousness and vomited twice. The banging George heard as he approached Stockbridge was not Jonny trying to get him to stop the car, it was a seizure which stretched and shook him, twisted his neck and forced his teeth like a clamp through his tongue. As the car rattled and rolled over the country roads, the pressure between his skull and brain built and built until a stroke paralysed the nerves in his face and the left-hand side of his body. Now, upon the quiet clearing of Ashton Peak Ridge, he was stuffed in the cramped trunk, drooling and blowing bubbles of blood, crooked but conscious, unable to blink, looking into the darkness.

George got out of the car. In the fresh night air, the treetops were silhouetted sharply against the cloudless moonlit sky, and at the bottom of the hill he could see the reflection of the moonlight on the rippled sea. He stood a moment, breathed deeply, and steeled himself to reason with Jonny; to persuade him that there was no need for him take revenge. Because revenge, George decided, had been Jonny's motive for going to the house. Revenge for using him, for taking advantage of him. Revenge for not taking him seriously. But George could talk him through. He was sure they could solve this. Jonny was young. Maybe this was his first heartbreak, which is always a terrible thing. No wonder he wanted to hurt him. But he was young.

'You are young,' he would say, 'and your life will move quickly. I am old and my years are like bars of a cage around me, but you are still free. You can have anything, and I'm stopping you. Let the momentum of your youth carry you, there is nothing holding you here. Nothing. Don't be afraid of moving on. Let life move you. It will. You are young.'

That was what he would say. That sounded good. Yes, he was sure they could figure this out. He would go back to Alice. There was a way through this for everyone.

A fox passed through the clearing, nose to the ground, stopped for a second and looked at him, then silently disappeared into the wood. George walked to the back of the car. He put the keys in the lock and opened the trunk.

BULLETS

Long before Alan moved away, me, Ronan and him collected bullets. There was a loose flagstone with a hollow underneath it, and we put the bullets in there. Our secret stash of gold. The artillery range was more than a mile from our little street. At the back of the terrace, the hill was covered with old woods. So many of the trees were twisted, the ground was dense and pitted, and we made thin paths around the mud holes and over rotten trunks. Up at the top there were the broken walls of an old castle. From there, where it levelled off at the top, was a flat field where the fences started. You could hear the snap of the guns, especially early in the morning. From the hedges at the edge of the field we'd hide and watch the men aim and crack and reload, and aim and crack and reload, and aim and crack and reload. When they finished and the vans drove away, we'd climb the fences and go to where they'd been shooting and scour the ground for shells. Not the empty cylinders, there were hundreds and hundreds of those, but the ones with the points still on. There were a lot fewer of these, but they were there, dropped carelessly in the rush to reload. With so many soldiers training, there were a lot of bullets to collect. When we got them, we brought them to the back alley behind our houses and put them under the flagstone. I think maybe Alan started it. He was the oldest. I never remember the hole being empty, and over the years the little collection grew and grew. It was our secret. That little pit of gold.

The first time I met Maddie was during the summer. I was seven. She was sitting on the footpath across the road, outside the Dempseys' house, playing with marbles. I wanted something to swap with her. I'd never seen marbles before. I ran out to the alleyway. I got my fingertips under the edge and bit by bit I lifted and dragged the heavy flat stone. I'd never done it alone before, usually there was at least me and Ronan doing this, and it slipped and scraped the concrete. As soon as the gap was big enough, I squeezed my hand into the blackness. The bullets were cool in there and rattled like boiled sweets in a bowl as I grabbed a handful. I knew that they were rare. She probably wouldn't have seen them before. I ran back through the house. My dad stopped me.

'What's in your hand?'

'Only something. I want to swap it for some marbles. I have a new friend. She's visiting the Dempseys.'

'Oh, the English girl. Show me.'

I hesitated.

'Connor, show me.'

I opened my hand.

'Jesus,' he said, 'give me those.'

* * *

Before lunch there were army vans and Garda cars blocking the street. There were men with guns guarding the end of the road, stopping the cars, leaning in at the windows. In the alley, the flagstone was up. The hole underneath was bigger than I'd thought. We'd never taken it all the way off before. It broke up the little alley and now men with helmets and big gloves crouched at the pit looking in. They looked like they were friends, like the way that Ronan and Alan and me did when we were putting the bullets in. If we were grown up, we'd be working together dressed like that. They were taking the treasure. Our treasure. I wanted to cry but I held it back. When they asked me, I said the same as I had said to Maddie and my dad. I didn't know how they got there; I just knew they were there. I said that Ronan and Alan had shown me, that we were the only ones who knew about it and no, we didn't know how the bullets had got there. They said they'd ask me more questions later. They never did. Some more people had come around now, curious about the army vans in the village. Me and Maddie sat on the footpath and watched. I'd never heard an accent like hers before, not even on TV. I remember she said, 'It's only my first day here.'

The news said that a store of bullets for an IRA cell had been found in a rural village. Earlier in the year a stash of guns and rifles had been stolen from a barracks across the border. They never found the guns, but now they had found the ammunition. Everyone said what a great job the Gardaí had done.

We kept that secret. Me, Alan and Ronan.

* * *

Maddie came back every summer. Her dad was a cousin of the Dempseys, and was in charge of the factory that was going to be built near the village. She had her hair in a high ponytail, and she wore t-shirts with logos, tucked into her shorts. She chewed gum and knocked on my door. We'd trek into the woods and swing from branches. We'd go up to the old castle. They didn't have old ruins like that where she was from, she said, they had big castles with flags on the battlements. How come it was a ruin? I didn't know. I'd never thought about it. The castle wasn't important. I just liked hearing her talk. We'd try and copy each other's accents. She told me about the Irish people in Nottingham. They were dangerous, she said. They collected scrap iron and raced dogs. Her mum told her to watch out for them. I didn't know any English people. Ronan's dad sang rebel songs. We could hear him from next door sometimes.

She started playing football with us on the road, but she kept her hands in her pockets. When we went to the village green and played there, she'd sit on the wall and watch. Sometimes, Mike, Ronan's older brother would wheel Brian to the green and leave him sitting there. Brian was the youngest and had always been in a wheelchair. We didn't know if he was watching the game or not, it was hard to tell. Ronan said he was born that way. That was why his dad was always singing. There was no point talking to Brian, he couldn't talk back, but he liked the songs, Ronan said. The songs were old, and he'd sing them over and over, but I could never make out the words. His voice was deep like an old farm engine and I grew used to hearing the run of a melody coming from next door. I'd forget about Mr Brady. The song was coming from the thick stone. The walls were singing.

One of those summers I had my first seizure. One evening on the village green. I just remember being pulled away, a sudden distance opening between me and everything around me, and then waking up on the ground. The light had changed. It was darker than usual. From the look on Alan's face I knew something was wrong. He'd never looked at me like that before. He was kneeling next to me and behind him, Maddie was standing with her hand to her mouth, looking pale. Ronan and Mick were crouched over me too. Brian was still in his chair near the wall, but no one was with him now. When I got to my feet I was aching, and my tongue was swollen. I wanted to know what time it was. Maddie was gone, she had run back to get my parents. While I waited, I sat on the wall. The village green was different, like it wasn't the real one anymore. That distance that had opened up, that change of light, remained. I felt like I was visiting. I waited for that feeling to go away but it never did. Summer was nearly over.

* * *

The village was growing. Fields were cleared and flattened. The little road had been widened, a new one was put down, and two new estates were being built. Fine white cement dust covered everything like a baker's board. The windows of the houses, the bushes, the broad leaves on the old trees all the way up into the woods, had all been sprinkled in a dirty white. Everyone on the street took to washing their cars, but as soon as they did, the cars were covered again. They couldn't do anything about it, it was just there in the air. When Maddie came back, we climbed up to the old castle again. The shell of the factory lay across the back of the village like a huge abandoned ship, and at the edges of the new estates were houses waiting to be finished, with empty windows and doorways like missing teeth. The children from new families that were moving in were all playing in these half-built houses, the boys running around with sticks from the old wood playing war and the girls on the driveways planning dance routines or making houses into girls only zones. By the time the younger ones were rounded up by their parents and the others were at the village green, we'd hang around there until the sun went down. I was on medication now, and the days were longer but still never as bright as before. On one of those long summer evenings, we kissed, Maddie and I, in a cold concrete corner of what became, before she left, someone's living room.

Almost as soon as she left, the factory opened. The school was suddenly full that year. Next door, Ronan's parents started fighting. His dad's voice changed. Before, I could hear him singing his songs through the walls. Now, voices hot and sharp, stripped the air. Mike and Ronan's voices joined in too, shouting their dad down. Mike was big now and he was out of school. He was working at the factory and drinking at the pub. During the cold winter and spring months, me, Alan and Ronan stayed out later and later. We'd steal cigarettes from our parents and smoke them on the corner of the new estate. If we were short, Ronan always had a stash, or we'd ask Mike for a few when he was on his way to the pub. Alan was the first one in the village to get a leather jacket. His dad had bought an old motorbike and was showing him how to fix it. We'd spend time in Alan's garage, while he'd take apart the metal jigsaw again and again before reassembling it and revving it, bringing it to life. Ronan never spoke about what was going on at home. I used to see his mum getting Brian in and out of the car. The only times I'd see his dad was when I called in. He'd be in the back room. There never seemed to be any light in that room, just the glow of the TV. From the hallway I couldn't see the screen, just Mr Brady on the sofa, illuminated in a shaky light. He never spoke to me. He'd only give a grunt. Upstairs, Ronan had a Walkman with big headphones. Mike's old comics were piled on the dresser and we'd read the comics and go through his tapes, taking turns with the headphones. Sometimes Ronan would be called to help, and we'd hear the wheelchair being moved around downstairs. I'd try to sound out the action noises in the comics – Whap! Booom! Ssshriing!

One night on the way out, his dad shouted at me and Alan, calling us into the front room. He was sitting on the sofa. There was a confusion of voices coming from the TV and the colours on his skin moved. Brian was sitting in his chair, motionless.

'You're hanging around with the English family, aren't ya?'

'Well, the Armstrongs. They're the Dempseys' cousins.'

'That English girl.'

'Yes.'

He pointed at me.

'Careful what you bring into your family boy, into this community.'

The light from the TV changed and now it shimmered on his face. The lines at the edge of his mouth and eyes were deep and sharp.

'Mr Brady…' but he cut me off with a grunt. He squinted. The lines moved in splinters, cut deeper. Brian moaned. Mr Brady didn't move; he was still pointing at me. Alan tugged at my sleeve. I didn't want to leave. I wanted to see it, I wanted to see him squint even more and see that ugly disapproval shatter his face. Alan tugged at my sleeve again and we left.

Outside, just before Alan turned to go his way home, he said, 'When Maddie comes over again, I'm going to ask her out. She likes me. She's nice, isn't she?'

'I kissed her.' I said

'How many times?'

'Just once.'

* * *

Then the summer came around and when I saw the car with the roof rack parked across the road, it felt like I had jumped and stayed in the air. All I wanted was to hear her talk again, and my impatience of mind was unbearable until she knocked. She had a new football. She stood at my door with it under her foot and a big smile. Soon Alan was playing with us on the village green. I went in goal and he and Maddie tackled and took shots. He had gotten better, he was faster. He was taller this year too. So was she. Her hair was longer and her tucked in white t-shirt was showing the shape of her chest now. I could see the straps of her bra underneath as she tackled the ball away from Alan and he chased her.

Later on, I heard Maddie promising she'd go and look at his new bike with him. He said he'd take her for a ride. Alan started hanging around with us all the time then. He asked Maddie all about Nottingham, about the differences between there and here. I heard her tell him about the castle in Nottingham right in the middle of the town. It wasn't a little ruin like ours. They walked together while me and Ronan kicked the ball around the road after them. I was sure there was an excitement in her voice. Alan was making her laugh more than I did. Because he was taller, the way she turned and looked when he spoke was different, and there was a way she held herself when she walked next to him. When I saw it, I felt a sickness, like the moment when you're climbing and you hear the branch snap. One day she told us about some bombs that were found near her street. If they had gone off, her street, her house would have been blown up.

'What's it got to do with me?' she asked. Alan nodded and touched her shoulder.

* * *

Some evenings she wouldn't call. When I went and knocked across the road and she wasn't there, I'd end up just sitting by my window so that I'd see her when she came back. My embarrassment when it was dark and she still hadn't walked through the door stuck in the air around me, I felt it push against me every time I turned around. It made my day an empty cartridge, hollow and useless. The thoughts of her with Alan kept me awake. It felt like I would never sleep again until I talked to her. On the day before she left, she called for me and we walked up through the woods beyond the old castle and sat on a fallen tree looking onto the flat field where they used to shoot.

'What was it like on the motorbike?'

'Oh, yeah. A bit too fast. He asked me to be his girlfriend.'

'Are you?'

She shook her head.

She leaned into me. We kissed. She tasted like gum.

'When you go back to Nottingham, do you have a boyfriend?'

'You're my boyfriend now, aren't you?'

* * *

Alan stopped going to school then. He worked in the local garage. On our way to school the shutters were open and we'd see his shadow and clouds of breath. On the way back we'd call in, and he'd lean up from under a bonnet or roll out from under a car and wipe his hands. Sometimes he'd take a break and share his cigarettes and we'd smoke. One day he was sitting sideways on his bike, his overalls covered in grease and he told us that his dad was going to pay for him to go to England to get work there. We smoked in silence for a while.

'Are you going to stay here and work in the factory?'

'Maybe. I don't really want to.'

'Everyone else around here is going to.'

'Exactly.'

'We should have held onto it.'

'What's that?'

'The pit of gold.'

We laughed.

'Did you ever tell anyone?'

'Oh no. Sure that's a good secret. Don't want to spoil that one.'

'That's long gone.'

Ronan said, 'I've still got a little stash.'

We all laughed some more and threw the cigarette ends on the floor of the garage. Alan left soon after that. He was gone by the summer.

* * *

The next time she came over, Maddie got a job packing in the factory. On the village green, a football league with teams from each estate started up. Soon, teams from other villages were coming to play during the holidays. We'd sit and watch them, and the other people on the green would shout and cheer and joke. The more noise they made, the less it seemed we needed to. The players' boots dug into the grass. The kicked-up soil and the scent of the earth in the evenings textured the thinning summer air. We held hands when we walked. I kissed her every night before we said goodbye. Ronan's mother left that summer too. He said that she had just been waiting until he and Mike could look after each other. She took Brian with her. Ronan got a little van and took every opportunity to get away from home. He took Maddie and me to the coast a few times. We'd sit for a while on the beach, but never stay long. Ronan didn't seem to have much to say anyway. The closer me and Maddie got, the further away Ronan seemed. Then we wouldn't see him for a while. He'd be gone for days, sometimes weeks at a time. His father stopped shouting and went back to singing rebel songs. Some nights after I'd said goodnight to Maddie and counted my medications, I would start thinking about how it would feel to be together, and there would be the voice, some old muffled stories about some kind of glory, coming from the walls.

Before she left that year, Maddie said she was going to move to Dublin to study. Ronan didn't go back to school. It was just me now, and I wanted to get it over with as soon as I could. I knew I could just keep my head down and work hard. School was nearly over. Summer was waiting for me, and like every summer since I was a boy, so was Maddie. I was eighteen. I got a job in the offices of a newspaper in Dublin. She had started at Trinity, studying International Law. We got a place together. She made a chart to put on the wall. I had to tick it when I had taken my medication.

'Just so I'm sure,' she said, 'I need to know you're not going to have one when you're on the bus or in the street.'

* * *

The next time I saw Ronan was six years later. I was back in the village and I saw his van outside. The local football team had made it to the county finals. The game was being played on the new pitch up on the hill. Everyone from the village and the new estates was out, walking to the game, already jubilant. The fact that the game was happening at all was a cause for excitement. There were banners proclaiming good luck, hanging from windows, and cars honked their horns. I called in. His dad was still there, in front of the TV in the dark back room. He grunted at me. I said, 'I'm going to marry Maddie Armstrong, Mr Brady, I'm going to marry her you know.' Ronan grabbed a pack of beers from the fridge and threw his coat on and pushed me back out the door.

We joined the throng.

'I didn't know there were this many people in the village,' Ronan said. 'Are you really going to marry her?'

'I think so. I haven't asked her yet. But I think we'll do it.'

'I bet she's even more gorgeous now. You hung on to her alright.'

'It's not even this busy in Dublin.'

'It's not even a big game.'

'Well, come on, county league final.'

'Yeah, but it's not much of a county.' He opened a can as we walked. Around us, groups of men with team shirts and scarves joined colours and followed the road out of the village until the crowd was thick. Someone had made a flag, and when it was hoisted and waved, a cheer resounded. The road wound up to the new pitch, onto the flat of land at the top where the supporters for the other team were gathering on the other side. By the time the teams came out of their dressing rooms, the side-lines were packed, and as soon as the ball was in play the noise back and forth was as much of a competition as what was on the field. I wasn't going to drink, but we finished

Ronan's six pack before the second half started. When the teams came back on there was still only a goal in it. Ronan produced a naggin from his inside pocket. He had stopped cheering long ago. Another goal halfway through and our crowd jumped and hugged and cheered like we'd made it to salvation day. One more goal and we'd all be there. Ronan supped from his naggin and leaned into me and talked right into my ear.

'Mike and Dad didn't know it, but I was seeing someone last year. From over the 'Cross. We've broken up now. It's such a fucker.'

The fans were really shouting from the sides now, throwing their arms about. The captain, a skinny player with a scraggly beard, kicked the ball right to the feet of a winger who rushed past two men and put it to the other wing. There was a scuffle and two men went down. The ball went out. Everyone was shouting at the linesman now as the players got up and pushed each other. The ref blew and it was our free. The captain roared and the team surged to the box.

'I couldn't tell her what I did.'

'What do you mean? What you did?'

'What I do.'

The free kick was cleared but we were on the attack again, but every time we tried to get through the ball was cleared, but we kept possession and kept setting up another attack. All the supporters on our side of the pitch were on the balls of their feet, dancing around the edge of a celebration. Voices clamoured – C'mon lads! – Go on! – Ref! – Go on boys!

'What I do.'

'Ronan– ' I wanted to tell him to shut up for a minute, Jesus, this was important, it looked like we were going to score. Of all the games played, this one could be the one that made the village proud. Players collided, the ball skimmed across the grass, was controlled – Your ball! – Watch the wing! Then a tackle brought it back – C'mon boys! – Mark him! – Get it in! It went to the wing – This is it! – Keep them out! – C'mon boys! – Guns Conor!

'Wait, what?'

There was a pass to the centre, another player ran in from the edge of the box, shouting for the ball.

'I've been working in a southern cell. Small one. Mostly dumping guns brought over the border.'

'Ah Jesus,' and there was the shot. I jumped, tight with everyone else, but the keeper put it out to the side and we all exhaled. I looked at Ronan. He was looking at the pitch now and sipped from his naggin as the players rushed forward again, jostled for position, back in the box. They looked fevered now and elbowed and pushed each other as the captain stepped back to take corner – Yes boys! – This is it! – Get it in! – C'mon! – This is it! Ronan was still looking ahead. The captain kicked it into the box.

'Mike and Dad don't know that either.'

We scored. There was a noise like a spike going through their crowd, and we exploded with long wordless sounds, sheer joy, faces reddened with triumph, fists beat the air and strangers exchanged fevered embraces. Within a minute, the whistle was blown, and we'd won, our little village had got to the top of the county. A torrent of triumph roared down the hill and celebration sang around the streets of the village. Everybody gathered in the green, drinking and cheering and laughing and chanting and toasting the provincial victory. We sat on the wall.

'I didn't think you'd do that. Guns, Ronan.'

'Well,' he said, 'and coke. They don't need so many guns now. And there's more money.'

'The girl from the 'Cross, did she find out?'

'No. I just couldn't tell her. You're lucky. You got lucky.'

We kept going back to the pub. We brought out our pints and sat on the village green wall, watching the celebration around us.

'Do you have some in the house now?'

'Guns?'

'Coke. Come on now. What would I want with guns?'

'Ah yeah. There's always a bit yeah.'

By the time we got back to Ronan's, I realised how drunk we were. I'd forgotten to take my key out, so Ronan said I could crash at his. The TV was on and his dad was asleep, sitting upright on the sofa. Ronan took me up to his room and opened the bottom drawer of the cupboard. He took out a handgun.

'This is mine.'

He handed it to me, and I held it for a while as he cut up a few lines on the dresser. It wasn't as heavy as I thought it would be. It could have been fake for all I knew. He inhaled.

'I've never used it.'

'Put it away.' I stood up and gave it back. I rolled up a note.

'Maddie takes care of you right?'

'Well, I mean, we take care of each other I think.' I covered one nostril and inhaled. 'It's like the dust from the old factory.' I dabbed a finger on the leftover grains.

'Let's go downstairs. We'll move the old man.'

We couldn't wake his dad. He was cold and his breath was weak. It was like a pencil scraping a desk. We tried to lift him off the sofa, but he was too heavy. His breathing stuttered. There was a gap, then a sound like twisting a bottle cap, then he stopped. We froze, holding him like that, and waited for it to come back. In that silence Ronan and me just looked at each other. Fear was filling the space where his father's breath should have been.

'Ah shit,' he said. 'Now look what's happened.'

'Call an ambulance Ronan,' I said, and we put him down on the sofa again. The breath returned. I could hear the thin stream of air, but it didn't seem like it was going in or out. Ronan was giving his address and rubbing his hand up and down over his face, tilting his head and checking his nostrils in the mirror and slapping himself on the back of the neck.

'Yes, I'll stay on the line'.

It took two weeks for Mr Brady to die.

* * *

The church wasn't full for the funeral. Mr Brady's friends were part of the old village, before the factory. I couldn't remember a time when he wasn't old. Me and Maddie were just two seats behind Ronan and Mike. His mum was there, with her partner, a lean, straight looking man in a well-fitted suit. Brian wasn't there. He was in a home, being cared for. As the casket was carried out, I saw Alan at the door. He had his suit jacket over his shoulder, his tie was slightly askew, his chest defined beneath his shirt. His hair was shaved and he had stubble that was thick and crept up to his cheekbones. He looked like it wasn't his suit, or maybe he'd been wearing it for days, but there was a solidity to him, a sense of consequence. We hugged. He hugged Maddie too.

'You guys, still together!'

'You look good Alan,' Maddie said.

There were tears in everyone's eyes when Ronan came out, he looked skinny and grey and streaked with grief, as if this wasn't the real Ronan, he was already gone. His mum and Mike walked behind him and held each other up. We walked with the procession to the graveyard behind the church. As they lowered him in the priest intoned a prayer. There was freedom to be found in the grave, rest which comes in the arms of the earth, an end to the struggle, peace at last.

'You still in England?' I said to Alan.

'On and off, I've been in the Middle East for a bit.'

'What have you been doing there? Still working on engines?'

'Not really, well, sort of. How's your health? Still on the meds?'

'Always.'

'But you're OK?'

'Oh yeah, fine. We're living in Dublin.'

'Good, good.'

He and Maddie walked together to the pub. She was telling him all about her studies and her job, all about Dublin. I stayed close to Ronan. Ronan's mother reminisced about the old village, the small school, the little shop, and about that time when they found the bullets under the flagstone. We didn't say anything about it. There was no point now, it felt so long ago. Later, Ronan said, 'Wasn't that Maddie's first day?'

After the pub emptied out, we went back to Ronan and Mike's. Though we clowned about and threw laughs and teased, the air had a heaviness of inevitable defeat. At the door, Mrs Brady didn't want to come in. Her partner said again how sorry he was, and then there was just us. We ended up in the back room, Maddie and

Ronan on the sofa, Mike on a chair and me and Alan sitting on the ground. A bottle was being passed around.

The talk turned and Mike asked Alan again what he was doing in the Middle East.

'I'm in the army,' he said. 'I've been sitting on top of a roof under a plastic sheet in the baking fucking sun and dust with my rifle, waiting for someone to walk out of a door. Twenty days.'

Maddie sat forward. 'What? You've been what?'

'What army, the British Army?' Mike said, 'The British Army?'

'In the Lebanon.'

'A sniper?'

'Sometimes. That's what I've just been doing.'

'Jesus.'

'I know.'

Ronan didn't sit up. He had his hand to his forehead holding his eyes closed.

'Did you get him?'

'What?'

'The target. Did you get him?'

'Turns out he wasn't there.'

'Or he got away without you knowing.'

'Yes.'

Ronan stood and crossed the room and looked down at Alan.

'British Army. Alan.'

Alan half laughed and put his hands up in surrender. 'I know. It's a strange world Ronan, it's a strange world.'

Ronan went upstairs.

* * *

Alan started to talk about how he got into the army, all of the training, how tough it was. Maddie asked what other things he did. Protect people, rescue fellow soldiers, combat, kidnap hostiles, wait a lot. Ronan had been gone a while. I stood up, patting Alan on the shoulder as I made my way upstairs. He was in his room, leaning over the dresser. He had a rolled-up note and was just about to sniff a line.

'Do you want some?'

'Sure, a little bit.'

He inhaled, and straight away set up another one. The top of the dresser was dark wood, the streak of powder glowed white. There was a little ornamental bowl and a glint of gold caught my eye as I took the line. I took a bullet from the bowl and looked at it. When I turned, he was sitting on the bed looking tired, resting the gun on his lap. I sat next to him. Alan was talking downstairs. We listened to the mumble.

'Would you've guessed?'

'Jesus no. I thought he'd be working in a garage, playing in a local football team, hitting on the English girls. I honestly thought that that was why he left. To get an English girl like Maddie. Is that loaded?' I turned the old bullet in my fingers.

'No. Well, a bit. Those are old rifle cartridges. Those old bits of gold. They're not for this.'

'All the things he's done, none of them have been over here. It's all in the Middle East.'

'Fighting in a country that isn't even his.'

'Well, leave him. It's not really fighting for anything is it? It's just fighting, Ronan, really. It's just an excuse to shoot a gun.'

'Conor, he's sitting in the room where my dad was. Dad's not even cold and there's a British Army Officer in our front room.'

'It's Alan. And Maddie.'

'And Maddie.'

'Ronan, you were mad at your old man, all the time, for the way he was. Weren't you? C'mon, we'll go downstairs.'

'I'm just going to line another one up.'

'I'll wait then.'

'And I bet he still hasn't got a girl like Maddie.'

'You're going to put the gun away?'

'Do you think he's killed anyone?'

'Yeah. Probably. Just, well, when I saw him at the church and now he's said it, it makes sense, the way he looked. He looked…'

'That's what I'm supposed to be doing isn't it? A rebel? Fighting? Isn't that what I'm supposed to be doing?'

'I don't know, Jesus, don't ask me. I just have word counts and medications, and I can barely get those right without Maddie looking out for me. But I know that that gun, it's just for show. Ronan. Come on. It's Alan. Alan.'

Ronan lined up another two thin rows of coke on the dresser and sniffed one. He put the gun into the belt of his trousers and covered it over with his shirt.

'Let's go,' and he went out the door and down the stairs.

Back in the room, Maddie and Alan were talking about England. Maddie was listing what her friends over there were doing. She missed it sometimes. Ronan stood there, took the bottle and started singing a rebel song. Mike joined in. Maddie and Alan fell silent. I went and sat next to Maddie, and said to her quietly, 'It'd be a good time for us to go.'

She shook her head and edged away from me. The brothers' voices were strong together, the song

138

increasing in volume as they continued through the verses. Ronan's eyes were filling with tears. Mike had his closed.

> O come, come from o'er the river, and raise thy
>   hands chained,
> Dark Rosaleen, though gentle are thy graces,
>   now your freedom unrestrained,
> Shall flow from e're our fathers fought and e're
>   our brothers died,
> And Ireland born anew united in blood will in
>   glory rise.

When they finished, Alan and Maddie clapped. I raised my glass. Mike stood and put his hand on Ronan's shoulder. Alan said, 'Your dad was a proud patriot, and was always good to everyone here in the village. Long may his memory last.' He picked up the bottle and went around the room filling a glass for each of us. We all stood. 'To Tom Brady!' We drank.

Maddie sat down again and said, 'Sing another, another one of your dad's songs.'

I sat, close to her. 'Maddie, we should go soon.'

She ignored me. 'Have you got any more Ronan? Any more of your dad's songs?'

Mike sat down. 'He used to sing to Brian all the time.'

'Were they all like that? Irish Army songs?'

'No, Jesus, no. That was the only rebel song he sang. And he hardly ever sang that.'

'Hang on, Mike,' I sat forward. 'I remember hearing him singing all the time, there were more songs than that. Sure, half the time it was when I was trying to go to sleep. And when your mum left, he didn't stop. I mean, he didn't just sing to Brian, did he? He'd sing half the night in an empty house.'

'But not rebel songs Conor.'

'What? Well what the hell was he singing then?'

Alan leaned forward and topped up my glass again. Maddie held out hers and he filled it too. He passed the bottle over to Ronan and Mike, before he sat cross-legged on the floor.

'Go on lads,' he said. 'Sing us another.'

Ronan started to sing. He had a voice like his dad's, a kind of a plodding, workman's tone, but a sure handle on the tune. He knew what he was doing with it. I knew this tune, it was a part of my growing up, the song through the walls in the evenings. The melody quickly came around to the start again. It was hypnotic, but for the first time I could hear the words. It wasn't a song that yearned for liberty or revenge or freedom. It was a love song. A song of a brief passionate love which had to be abandoned, a love unfulfilled but that lives on in the song, and the song will be sung, and the love will live on. A song of the heart. By the end, Maddie and Alan were crying. And Ronan didn't stop. He sang another, and with each song he revealed another story which I'd thought I'd heard, songs I thought I knew, but I never knew really. And they were all about love. About tenderness. About innocence. Love. That's what he'd been singing about.

Ronan sang Raglan Road. He sang about Nancy Spain, the Parting Glass, the Galway Shawl, he sang The Star of the County Down. We stayed there till dawn.

DIGGING

I'm nearly home. My shopping is heavy; three bags a hand and that's when I see him digging. He's up to his waist, in the middle of the garden, and in a concentrated rhythm he bends then digs, straightens and tips, the earth slides and piles on the grass, and then he bends and digs again. I walk down the path. Neither of us acknowledges the other. The shopping strains on my wrist, the plastic is stretching as I reach the lock with the key and push open the door and he still bends and digs, straightens and tips and bends and digs. Once inside, I peer back through the window. He continues to dig.

* * *

And that was the dream. I dreamt it exactly like that for three nights running.

I told my youngest son about it. Of all the children, he'd be the one who'd be most interested. Even when he was a little boy, a chubby happy boy, he'd plan stories for his dreams. He was always awake much later than the others. Once I walked out of the living room and there he was, sitting half-way down the stairs.

'How did you get down here?' I said.

Evan got off the sofa and stood next to me. For a moment we just stood there, taking it in. I could tell Evan didn't want to make a big deal of it.

'You got down yourself? Let's see if you can do that in the morning. I'll bring you back up now, time to go to sleep now.'

'I've got some good ones,' he said. He wanted to tell us all about them.

'No,' I said, 'you tell us about the dreams after you've had them you little monkey. Well done for making it all the way down. Now let's see if you can come down these stairs by yourself in the morning.'

He did. He started moving about by himself then. Slowly, but he was managing. He was a terror for wanting to stay up. He'd say anything.

One night he said, when Evan picked him up for bedtime, 'Ah, but I am asleep Daddy. This is my dream now, so you don't have to take me up.'

Another night he asked how come he could remember things that had never happened.

'Imagination or something,' I said, 'now go to sleep.'

'Imagination. When I grow up, will I remember me running?'

Well, now he suggested that I try to interact with the digger. To ask him who the grave is for, if it is a grave. I can't make conscious choices in dreams, I said. There was a slight delay on the phone because he was in New York. After a second or two of silence he said, so make subconscious choices. You keep having the dream for a reason, maybe you're supposed to meet this guy. I needed to tell myself over and over before I went to sleep that I would talk to the digger. I needed to tell myself that I'd observe everything in the dream and ask the digger what I wanted to know. Look around you in the dream, he said, there may be something else you're missing.

He was in New York to work with a producer. It was a pilot, a one-man show he'd written. The producer couldn't afford to pay the full studio fee, so they worked on studio down time. That meant the middle of the night. It wasn't all his money, he had a backer, someone else from the States, who was willing to invest in the pilot, but not so much that they could work during the day it seemed. So he was working through the night. I asked him what he did in the day. He said he'd found a great bar that was open in morning. He went there after the studio before going back to his friend's apartment to sleep while his friend was at work. So, in the mornings he went to a bar and, knowing him, probably got drunk. When he lived with me, after the break-up, he got drunk a lot. One evening, I remember, it wasn't a birthday or a big game day or anything, it was a Tuesday, he was drunk, and had been since the afternoon.

'Can you believe this is all legal? As much as you want!' he said, coming back from my drinks cabinet with another full glass. I remember his lopsided walk and the look of concentration on his face as he avoided the coffee table but spilled the glass over himself and then laughed and laughed and laughed. My son, with his bent leg and little arm, on the streets of New York at nine in the morning, drunk. That's how I pictured him. I worried about him, out amongst all those sober New Yorkers, all starting their day, going about their business, and this one drunken lopsided young northern lad just about getting out of their way, spilling his drink and laughing. I made him promise to call me. He called me once in two weeks. Until I told him about my dream. Now he called me every day.

* * *

I look up and down the terraced street to see if anyone else is around. It's empty. No parked cars even. My shopping is heavy. He's still digging. I want him to look at me, but he just bends and returns, depositing dark earth, mechanically. These are the only movements he has. I step off the garden path, on to the grass, towards him.

* * *

'Fantastic!' he said after a little pause. 'You broke the routine of your dream.' But it didn't help. I wasn't sure even if it was the same man digging. I'd started to think that every night it was a different man. I couldn't remember the face, whose face it was. My son said not to worry, that it would be a slow process. He was enjoying the story arc. His view of the world was always through some kind of hero's story. There always had to be a goal, something to overcome, something to fight for, heroes and villains, a struggle, a climax and a resolution.

I asked him about the pilot. It was going well. Another few sessions and they'd be done. The producer was sure that they'd get some interest. That night I told myself over and over before I went to sleep that I wanted to discover who the man was.

* * *

The only noise is his spade splitting, a sharp crunch, a dull drag and then slick earth spilling off the spade. I stand still with the heavy shopping straining at my wrist. I can't even hear his breath. It's just the rhythm of the spade in the earth, the strike and slide, getting deeper and deeper. Though I'm looking at the man, his strong arms, his dark hair and his thick neck, I can't see his face clearly. His hair doesn't obscure it, he's not hiding, but

144

his face just won't come into focus. I'm looking straight at him, but I can't see who he is. I step off the path, onto the grass. My garden has changed. It's the garden of the last house I lived in. That box that my mess of a marriage with Evan was kept in. Serene and tended from the outside, but don't open it up and look inside. My lush purple lavender bushes and rows of golden lilac are gone, there are just overgrown untended verges scattered with daisies and dandelions, dead plants in pots and trays, never planted.

* * *

He was eager to hear how the dreaming was progressing. When I told him about the garden, he said that it could be the death of the marriage, and that I was moving on. I should be happy. It was a very positive dream.

'It's just the kind of thing I could write about,' he said. 'Would you mind? I need something else to write about anyway.'

'How about the show?' I asked. There was a longer pause than usual. It turned out that the backer had seen the rushes and decided against the project unless it was radically changed. He was pulling his funding.

'What will you do now?' I asked.

'Go to the bar.'

'Be careful, New York is dangerous you know.'

'Mum, you've never been to New York.'

I went out into the garden and stood where the digger stood. I looked at the path. I looked at the door. I tried to see it like the digger would. If he saw it over and over… here she comes again with her heavy bags, any moment she'll walk along the path, keys in hand, looking at me nervously. Will she go straight to the door, will she try and talk, what is it she wants? What is–the phone rang. By the time I got inside it had stopped.

* * *

The garden is my own again, the grass is lush and short. I don't step off the path this time. He's digging continuously, smoothly, efficiently, there's nothing stiff about his movement now. I call to him. But instead of saying, 'Who is that grave for?' like I have rehearsed I hear myself say, 'What do mean? My son is in New York. Do you mean?' The man looks directly at me. His eyes are a bright blue and his cheekbones are high and defined. His skin is tanned and glistening with sweat. He's my father and although he looks nothing like the man I remember, I know that's who he is. He wipes a muddy hand across his brow, leaving a smear of dark fresh earth. My father came back from the war and he was old. His body was peppered with shrapnel. He couldn't work. He didn't want to go outside. He wanted everything to be quiet. When we were playing out on the street sometimes, I saw him look through the window. But in my garden, he's strong and he's busy. He continues to dig. 'My son is in New York,' I repeat. I continue along the path to the front door and lift the key to the lock. The shopping bags are heavy in my hands. I unlock the door and push it open. I turn around to look at him again. I wake up.

* * *

For the sixth day in a row, I talked to my son. It had been years since we'd spoken so often, not since he lived with me after his father and I broke up. I told him about the man, my father, and I told him that I couldn't ask him the question, and that he didn't say anything anyway.

'But you spoke to him!' he said. 'Ah, it would have been great to find out who the grave is for.'

'I'm tired of it,' I said, 'and why does it have to be a

146

grave? Don't people dig to find? Or just dig anyway? It's not always about burying. Why do you care so much?' I didn't want to keep dreaming this dream. Seeing a man who wasn't my father as my father had upset me. And I was angry at my boy. Why did he care so much? He could have it, let him have it. And then, in the next instant I was angry at myself for being angry at him. The phone was hot in my hand. I just wanted to be rid of the whole thing. I didn't want to see who he became the following night. I was tired of analysing the scene; it was filling my days as well as my nights. The dreaming was exhausting me. When I asked why the backer had pulled out, I could hear his own anger underneath his voice.

'I'm not commercial enough. He thought I was something else. I think he doesn't know how to sell me. It's my legs and this stupid arm. He's sent another script through. Carl said he'll produce it. But it's terrible. Terrible.'

When I suggested he give the new script a chance, the anger rose up and he snapped at me, 'Mum, you haven't read it, so you don't know what you're talking about.'

'You're there to act though, aren't you? And it could lead to something. Can you give it a chance? Do you have to take it so seriously? Should you take what you can get for the moment, and be happy with that?' Maybe being happy meant letting go of what it is you really wanted. But I couldn't tell him that. You can't tell a child they can do anything, be anything, and then when they're older tell them to forget all that if they want to be happy. But that was all I wanted; for him to be happy. The silence on the line was longer than usual. I felt a tremor of panic. I thought he was going to hang up.

'You're dead sweet Mum.' His voice was calm

147

again. The tremor disappeared. 'I'm through with it anyway, I'm going to write about your dream; tell me more about it.' So we talked some more about the dream. I was just happy to be chatting again. If he ever did write about it, he would change it anyway I was sure; introduce some element of suspense or threat, or make it more beautiful or tragic in some way. He wouldn't give me a straight answer when I asked him what he was going to do now in New York. I wanted him to come home, but I couldn't say that. He wanted to talk about my dream. I was tired of it; he could have it. You can't control a dream. That night in bed I told myself over and over that my son would be safe and successful. Over and over.

* * *

The street is empty; everything is still, but I can hear the hum of distant traffic and birdsong in the air. The shopping is heavy, the plastic is straining. Rhythmically, he bends and straightens up. Split crunch drag spill split crunch drag spill. He's waist deep. The garden grass surrounding him is long and unkempt. 'Is that a grave?' I say. He stands straight and looks at me. He's the same man as the previous night, but he's not my father now. His eyes are glassy. He leans back, resting on the wall of the hole. 'Did you get dinner?' he asks. I look down at the bags. They're full of cans and bottles. I put the bags down. A strange feeling, I feel dizzy for a moment, and I'm floating slowly up. The digger is looking at me lazily, his head tilting back as he follows my ascent. The garden is bigger than I remember, and there's the hole. He's standing in it, and he looks pretty tired of digging. I'm not surprised, the hole is big, much bigger than I'd thought. It can't be a grave unless he's going to bury us all. Only the perimeter has the grass and the blooms, the golden lilac and purple lavender blooming, such rich colours so early in the season, and as for the rest, he's dug it all up, it's just earth. There's a breeze and a soft thick texture of Spring air supporting me as I drift up, further away from my house, from the man. I see the gardens of my neighbours and in each, there is a hole with a pile of earth at its side, and I'm floating, with my keys in my hand, slowly and gently upwards and away from them all.

HOTEL ARGO

The desert heat was unforgiving. It was 40 degrees when the bus pulled up at Hotel Argo. The forecourt was parched and scorched. Thin grey weeds were growing and dying in the cracks, and there was a small sun-blanched fishing boat leaning on its shallow hull in the corner. The hotel was pale, and mostly long and flat, moving up to two stories at its edges, so that through the grimy glass of the bus it looked like a desolate half-buried H. Mr Cheever pulled up the handbrake and considered it. It looked closed. Like it had been closed for a long time. He gathered his old brown shoulder bag, stepped out of the bus and walked across the forecourt. The kids in the bus watched him disappear through the shadow of the main door.

Cheever, relieved to be out of the heat, took a breath of the cool air of the lobby and stood for a moment, wiping his glasses clean on the end of his shirt. When he put them back on, he saw Derra for the first time. Derra was leaning on the front desk, picking dumplings from an oily bowl and popping them into his mouth, looking straight back at him. Cheever said, 'Hello' and Derra responded 'Hello' and Cheever stepped closer and said, 'Do you speak English?' and Derra responded to that with 'Yes. I enjoy it, no problem' and then he pushed the final dumpling into his mouth and gestured for Cheever to come closer.

'Do you have any rooms?'

'Do you have a booking sir?'

'No, actually, I was – we were booked into Hotel Varulca, but there was a mix up with, well, with the booking and they couldn't fit us in, so, no, I don't. Do you have any rooms? We're a big group. Nine. Just one night.'

'Yes. Vurluca.'

'Yes, Vurluca.'

'Ah yes. Well Mister…'

'Cheever.'

'Mister Cheever,' he nodded. 'You should never trust a woman whose name you cannot pronounce. Now. Rooms. Let me see. Nine.'

'We don't need nine rooms, just for nine…' Derra waved his hand and opened a large ledger on the desk. With his oily fingers he slowly turned page after page. Besides the two of them in this hallway, there was no life here, the shutters on the front windows were pulled down. Some light bled onto the windowsills. It was all very clean.

Derra was tapping on the keyboard of the computer now with one hand and clearing his gums of dumpling dough with the other. Eventually he looked up to say, 'Yes it seems that luck lives here Mr. Cheever. How many rooms?'

'We have a group of eight, well, nine including me. So, I need a single and then the kids can share. Are they twin rooms? How many rooms do you have?'

'Kids? Really? That's a lot of kids. And just one of you. What age are the guests?'

'Seventeen, eighteen. They're good kids, really, you don't have to worry about them at all. Really.'

'Seventeen and eighteen. So young adults, Mr Cheever? Maybe the kids in your country stay kids longer than ours. And you are their only guardian? Boys and girls? So no double beds?'

'Yes. And the boys and girls will be in different rooms of course.'

'Of course. Well, Mr Cheever, you are lucky.' Derra looked up from the ledger with a wide smile. 'We have four twins and a double.'

'No singles?'

'The one available is with a double bed. You will have that.'

'OK. OK, well, yes. Let's do it. Thank you. And you are?'

'Derra. Welcome to Hotel Argo.'

* * *

The first thing that Becky noticed when they pulled in was the cats. White cats, with bright blue eyes. There, at the sides of the forecourt, in the thin shade of the wall, sitting, lying down and thinly slinking. Cheever had left the engine running, so no one wanted to get out of the air-conditioned bus. Except Becky. The smell of the bus after a week and a half was difficult, so much sweat and food and sun lotion. She opened the door and stepped into the hot air baking the forecourt. The boat was incongruous, sitting there, tilted. There were cats behind it, she was sure of it. She started to walk towards it when Mr Cheever came out with his thumbs up, saying, 'OK, we've got somewhere!' and with a tumbling noise everyone piled out of the bus and grabbed their bags. The cats scattered.

* * *

The first thing Becky and Sam did was check what room the other was in. Becky was in room twelve and Sam was in room twenty, at opposite ends of the corridor. Everyone was on the ground floor. Derra had told all of them, one by one, as they checked in, after he told them dinner and breakfast times, that the stairs at the end of the corridors were not safe, and that access to upstairs was prohibited. There is structural work going on, he said, this is an old building, and he repeated, it's not safe. As soon as everyone was checked in and had their keys, he went to the east wing of the hotel and up the stairs along the dark corridor until he came to room forty-four. He gave a brief knock and waited. The door then opened slowly and the big bent lumbering shape hissed and moved back across the room to the corner where a nest of blankets lay.

'We have visitors,' Derra said. 'I'll bring you your food. Don't leave the room. They will leave tomorrow. No one will come upstairs. I will bring you your food. Keep your door closed. I'll be back soon.' He turned and left, closing the door behind him.

* * *

At dinner, the kids lined up and Derra served out plates of thick brown meat and dumpling stew, and hunks of bread.

Cheever was last in line. 'Thank you Derra,' he said. 'You cooked this too? As well as prepare the rooms? Do you do everything?'

'Mr Cheever, I am the potato.'

Cheever looked blankly at him. 'The potato.'

'You don't have this in your country?'

'Well yes, we have potatoes, but…'

'It's a saying here. The potato can do anything. You

know? You can boil it, fry it, bake it, grill it, or roast it, it can be a soup or a French fry, it can be chopped, mashed, cubed, skin off or skin on, and the skin, well even the skin is used for eating. One potato, just one potato can feed more people than any other vegetable. There is more energy packed into a potato than any other vegetable. It will survive anywhere. They are growing potatoes in space Mr Cheever. You get the idea?'

'You are the potato.'

'Yes. Here, I am the potato.'

* * *

The group filled the tables. The stew was thick, with soft dumplings and lumps of stringy meat. The group, however, were hungry, and to Cheever's surprise, there wasn't a lick of food left on the plates once they rose to go.

He stood and raised his hand and his voice. 'Listen up gang, it's a curfew of eleven tonight. In the meantime, if there are any issues, I'm in room seventeen, come and see me. Mr Derra will be...' Derra was walking between the tables, collecting the plates. He didn't look up, just waved his arm in a circular motion above his head. 'Well, he'll be around. Please everybody, now, wait, listen. Don't go wandering. As you saw from our drive here, there's nothing around. It's just a long road back to Hotel Vurluca. It'll be dark by ten and by then, I want everyone back inside. Stay within the hotel perimeter. I'll be doing head checks. OK. This is the last night and it's been good, hasn't it? It's been a really great trip so don't mess it up.'

When they were walking out the door he sat down and took off his glasses and rubbed his eyes. His face was covered with a sheen of sweat. The sun was getting lower, but the heat was not abating. Presently Derra sat beside him and lit a cigarette. They stayed there in silence for a while before Cheever said, 'Have you got a bar here?'

Derra nodded and stubbed his cigarette out in Cheever's plate.

'First, I must do one thing,' he said, 'then if you want you can help me with the plate cleaning. Then I'll open the bar.'

* * *

Becky and Sam were alone together in room twenty.

Becky said, 'Do you still have it?'

Sam took the little plastic pouch from the inside pocket of his bag. 'Oh boy, everything stinks, ugh. Here.' He waved the pouch in front of Becky. She grabbed it from him.

'Are we going to take it all?'

'Well, I'm not carrying that through customs. But it's not much. We either take it all or just some of it, then throw the rest away.'

She spun around and threw herself backwards onto the bed. 'We'll have to find somewhere we won't be disturbed.' Outside their door, Derra passed along the corridor with a pot of stew and climbed the stairs. Sam sat beside her, and she sat up and kissed him then walked to the window. She could see that at the back of the hotel, the other kids had grouped around the pool. They'd taken down the old sun loungers from a stack in the corner and set them up. White cats sat underneath the bushes, watching. Becky saw a flash of blue when one looked at her through the window. Some of the kids were getting into the pool, clothed, disappearing from view, only to reappear and climb out, dry. The pool was dry, empty.

'That won't be hard.' Sam moved behind her and put his arms around her waist and took the pouch from her hand. 'There's got to be somewhere in this forgotten place where we can get high.'

Outside their door Derra passed again, without the pot.

* * *

The shutters on the small bar counter slid up smoothly then clicked, and Derra stood there for a moment, rubbing his hands on his shirt front, looking at the bottles.

'Have you had a good time in our country Mr Cheever? That's a lot of teenagers for just one person,' he said.

'Ah, they're OK. They're good kids.'

Derra chose a bottle and checked how much was left in it before crouching beneath the bar and getting two glasses.

'You can trust them?'

'I don't expect anything except for them to stay safe. So, yes, I think I can trust them not to do anything really stupid.'

'A little stupid is OK.'

'We all do stuff that's a little stupid. It's more important that they trust me. What have we got here?'

'This, Mr Cheever, is a piece of heaven in a bottle. Take it slowly.'

He poured and the two men clinked glasses and began to drink.

* * *

The sun was disappearing from the sky now, and the kids were outside, gathered around and in the empty pool, smoking and drinking the beers they had left over before leaving day. The laughter in the pool echoed and shouts bounced around the walls. Alan had found a metal pole and was in the middle of the empty pool, dancing and grinding around it while Beanie lay underneath him keeping the pole upright and straight. The others were on the edge, their feet dangling into where the water should have been, laughing and calling, 'Off, off, off!' Suzie climbed down and stuck a note in the waistband of his shorts and there were loud cheers as he peeled his t-shirt off. As the darkness fringed the edges of the sky and the air started to settle and cool, the shadows behind the pool started to fill with more skinny white shapes with bright blue eyes glinting like sapphires in the shadows.

* * *

'Well this place,' Derra drawled as he poured another glass, 'as you can see, isn't doing so well. They built a new road you see, years ago, and now we are out of the way of everything. The shops here closed, the petrol station. No one lives near here now.'

'Except you.'

'Except me. In this place. Well someone has to be here.'

'You can't sell it?'

'Let me tell you about this place. Many many years ago, long before the new road, it was owned by a couple, a lovely couple, they are old now, very old, dead now but it was the best hotel in the province. But she took an illness. They had to move to the city so that she could get regular medical help. But they did not sell. She couldn't bear to leave her cats you see. He would drive her back, across the island, anytime she said so, because she needed to see the cats. So the staff worked and they still owned it, that's when I started to work here. I'd see them sometimes, they were old even then, and she would come and visit, and the cats would come to her. She would not sell it for the cats. Then they built the road. This big road in a wide circle away from here. Things started to get bad. No trade. So he got ill and quickly died. And she was stuck in the city with her sickness getting worse. All she wanted was to be here with her cats. There was a son, all this time, but they couldn't give this place to him. He was taken by a fever when he was young, when he was a child and went crazy, very crazy, and so there you go. So I am here now. When she got sick, I made a promise to her. And the agreement with her, the promise was that I would stay and look after the cats.'

'But if she's gone, do you still have to do it? Can't you just sell and leave? She's gone after all.'

'Mr Cheever there is much you don't know about our country. A promise is a piece of you saved for tomorrow.'

* * *

Upstairs, Becky and Sam pushed the door and went into room forty-three together. It was dark. The lights outside shone through the window and the noise from the others bounced off the side of the building. Sam wiped the windowsill clean and Becky set up two lines.

'And this is coke for sure?'

'I hope so. He did say cocaine when I bought it.'

Becky dabbed her finger in the bag and put it to her tongue. A smile spread across her lips. She rolled up a note. On the other side of the thin wall something was stirring.

* * *

It was dark by now and Beanie was drunk, at the deep end of the empty pool. Everyone else was inside; all of the beer was gone, and he lay there, singing to himself and looking at the stars. The skies here are so clear and the stars so bright, he thought, maybe I could move here. Find a job, on the beach teaching surfing or running water sports, learn the language, find a beautiful island girl who would only need to wear a bikini all the time and I would get ripped and tanned and we'd get a place near the beach. I'd eat fresh fish and those fried dumplings with cheese and shrimp inside. I'm starting to feel hungry again. I could sit up but then it's nice like this. Since the first time I got drunk at my parents' garden party just before they broke up, I've been getting better and better at it. Then he saw a cat slink up beside him. He reached his hand over to stroke it. It flinched back, then came closer. He made kissing noises with his mouth and then saw another beside it. Aw, how cute. They came closer. He sat up. All around him the bottom of the pool was full of white cats, all of their blue eyes on him, all moving towards him. He held his breath for a second then started to gibber wordless noises, and went to get up, but there were cats on the edge of the pool too and they jumped down onto his head and shoulders. There was a sudden flurry and hissing and he never got the chance to stand up. Before he could do it, they had covered him.

* * *

Derra was pouring another drink. Cheever turned in his chair.

'It'll just be the cats. Something scared them probably or they caught something.'

Cheever turned back and checked the time.

'Cigarette?'

'No thanks.'

'So what is it you teach Mr Cheever?'

'Geology. Landscape, rocks, structural Geography. That's why we came here to see the Pillars of Janu. I came twenty years ago as a student. I wanted these students to see for themselves. They are truly amazing. I wanted to give the students what I had all those years ago.'

'Yes. Impossible structures. They are. Do you know who Janu was?'

'Yes, I know the legend. Janu the hero, of course. The north is quite amazing, the landscape.'

'Yes. And much cooler.'

'I wasn't expecting it to be so hot, so dry down here.'

'Yes. We are basically the desert of the country. On the other side of the mountains to the east there is more, but here there is not so much life. But they say in the desert if you live, you live the longest.'

They drank in silence for a moment while Derra smoked and tilted his glass back and forth.

'And the story of the hero Mr Cheever. Which one do you know?'

'The sisters of the Pillars. Wasn't it that Janu protected the sisters from Brovllanta, is that right? Brovllanta?'

'Brovtalla.'

'Sorry, yes, Brovtalla. Janu put the sisters in his protection so that they would survive because the warlord had promised to kill them, but then Brovtalla fell in love with them and because they would not, well, submit to his desires, he turned them into stone. Is that right?'

'Yes, indeed. That is the story. There is a word for that, the action of Janu. Do you have one in English?'

'For what?'

'In our language it is sisventisal. It describes the action of someone who has tried to make things better but through this has made things much worse.'

'No, I don't think we have a word for that. But I do love the story. I love the stories man makes to justify the land, the myths.'

'Myth.'

'Yes, all over the world, it's fascinating. The stories of Gods and heroes and monsters that man makes before the knowledge of science.'

'Hm. But you have the knowledge.'

'Not just me, we all do, we can all access it. It's easy to learn, it's easy to believe. It makes sense. It's an easier story than the myths.'

'Yes. Of course. And there are no monsters in the science, Mr Cheever?'

'No Derra. No monsters.'

'Mr. Cheever, let me tell you something.'

Derra let out a long thin string of smoke and examined the burning end before pressing it into the ashtray. 'Even when there are no monsters, there are monsters.'

* * *

Upstairs the little baggie was empty, and Sam and Becky were getting undressed in the little bathroom. A shower seemed like a good idea, they could close the door so the light wouldn't be seen from outside and it was small enough for them to have to be pressed together. Warm water sprayed from the old shower and steam started to fill the little room and fog the mirror as they kissed with numb lips and enjoyed the water running over their bodies. They rubbed the little soap bars, the size of a piece of candy, into each other, their skins slippily touching together. Then Sam stopped and said, 'Shh' and beneath the sound of the running water there was a loud creak from the room. When they heard the door open, they both froze, looking into each other's eyes and before they could turn around, the light turned off and a hissing sound sprang from the darkness. Then Becky screamed and through the steam, a misshapen form rose before them.

* * *

Downstairs, the group were in the lounge area. Alan and Prince were wrestling on one of the sofas, making a big deal of gaining control of the remote control. Cars were racing round a dirty track on the TV, throwing up red clouds as they swivelled around bends, with little people waving from the other side of a skinny rope, but Alan wanted to find an adult channel and he shouted about tits while glancing over at Suzie and Rachel. Suzie wasn't interested. She was on the other sofa frustratedly scrolling on her phone, just like Froggie at the opposite end. Rachel had found a tourist map and it was spread out on the ground in front of her. Cheever entered and counted.

'OK. Sam and Becky. Who knows where Sam and Becky are? They probably need to be interrupted. Alan, Prince, can you go find them, check their rooms, interrupt them and bring them back here. There's no signal here, so just go and get them. We're missing Beanie too. Where did you guys last see him? Suzie, Froggie? You know there's no point with that. Guys?'

Suzie and Froggie didn't look up from their phones,

Rachel didn't look up either, just traced her finger over the map. 'We're in the middle of a dried-up delta. Why does nothing grow here, shouldn't this whole area be a deposit of all the river mineral? A reptile sanctuary. An old mine. Is this a goat path or a walking path or something? I mean, who would come here?'

'Us. And we'll be gone tomorrow. It's time Rachel, it's all to do with time. OK, Alan, Prince you go outside and find Beanie. If he's not there, check the kitchen.' He sat on the arm of the sofa. 'It's all salt and heavy chalk deposits from the mountains. If you look you can see how the river has changed its course, see, there's another dry delta there, west. But it's all time. The river stopped running a long time ago. Now, Suzie, Rachel go to the rooms and get the lovebirds. Then come back here and we'll go over the plan for tomorrow and the airport.'

Prince pushed Alan backwards over the sofa and tossed the remote at him. Alan landed with his legs in the air much to the amusement of the girls. Alan got up and grimaced at them and followed Prince down the corridor. Becky and Suzie went the other way. Cheever sat down on the sofa and looked across at Froggie.

'You looking forward to getting home?'

'Oh yeah. Ten days feels like a long time.'

'Well, we've done a lot. These ten days will count for a lot down the line.'

'I guess.'

'There's a whole lot of future down that line. How about with the others? The last two days? Have things been better?'

'Yeah. No, not really. We just don't get on. Except Rachel maybe. But it's OK, it's no big deal. Just one more year of this and then there's a whole lot of future down that line.'

'Good man. How about the beer? Is that all gone now?'

'Beanie helped with that. I don't drink.'

'Yeah, I know, and I knew–' a noise, some kind of shout and hissing snapped their heads around.

'Was that from outside?'

'I think so.'

They both got up and ran through the lobby.

* * *

Upstairs, Suzie and Rachel were whistling and calling as they opened door after door. The rooms downstairs were empty, but they did find two more beers in Beanie's bag, so now they were swigging them in the dull light of the upstairs corridors and the checked room thirty-nine, room forty, forty-one, forty-two…

* * *

It was still heavy and hot outside as Cheever and Froggie walked to the pool. In the dark it was hard to tell, but it looked there were some empty beer bottles, the pole and at one end there were dark smears running up the pool wall. A few ghostly cats sleeked at the bottom, some of them sitting and licking themselves, their paws, each other.

'They're not here. The kitchen? Or maybe they've found the bar.'

'But what was the noise?'

'Let's try the kitchen.'

They turned and went towards the kitchen. The rest of the cats were beyond the fence, moving silently in a silver crescent following the running form of Alan, who was stumbling and sweating and falling on the rocky ground, then rising and running again. He was calling

over his shoulder, but his voice was smothered in the
darkness of the desert before it reached the hotel.

* * *

When they opened the door, Derra was there with an
apron, at the cooker with a large pot in front of him.
Large tuber shaped vegetables were stacked up on the
counter and he was chopping them and throwing them
in the pot. He turned lazily and Cheever could see the
spots of blood on his apron.

'Have you seen the boys?'

There were spots of blood on his arms too. And on
the floor.

'No, Mr Cheever, I have been preparing breakfast.
You leave after breakfast? For the airport?'

'We don't know where one of the boys went, well,
three of them now. One of them is drunk. Is there
anywhere else they could go?'

'Well Mr Cheever, seems like you have lost control
of your pack. The boys could have taken a walk outside,
but they will be back soon if they did. There is nothing
outside. Maybe at the front of the hotel?'

'Well, it's very strange, they went out the back. And
there were strange noises.'

'Noises.'

'We will go and look some more. I don't see any
meat Derra, what are you making? More stew?'

'The meat is in the pot. A local delicacy. The same
as you had earlier. Everyone enjoyed that, no? Out here
we have one dish that is best.'

'We'll keep looking. They might even be back in the
lounge. Come on Froggie.'

'Here, I will help you. Just let me put this on.' He
put down the knife and took another pot, pouring the

watery contents into the big pot and bending over to adjust the flame. 'You cannot let the pot go dry.'

* * *

Becky and Suzie opened the door of room forty-four and the first thing they saw was the discarded clothes on the floor. They heard the running of the water from behind the toilet door and there was steam creeping out from around its edges. Becky put her finger to her lips and Suzie giggled and they moved slowly, careful not to make a noise, through the dull light towards the glowing outline of the door.

* * *

In the kitchen, Derra untied the apron from behind his back and pulled it over his head.

'OK. We will go.' Then he shook his head and said, 'Wait…' he pulled the apron back over his head again, '…actually…' he picked up his knife again, '…I'm not finished.'

He stepped forward. Froggie turned and ran out the door, but before Cheever could get away, he was stopped by Derra thrusting the point of the knife at his throat.

'Derra, Derra… wait…'

* * *

Froggie was running through the lobby when he heard the screams from upstairs. They were high, loud, and they split the air. This was the first time he had ever heard real screaming. Screaming that froze then squeezed then shattered the core of him. The last terrifying noise before a terrible death. It stopped and then the sound of someone beating the floor, or the walls, or crushing the bed followed. As he ran, the hotel pumped with each rapid thump and then he was outside in the dust and the heat and the darkness.

* * *

The screams reached Cheever and Derra too, and Cheever felt himself start to shake. Derra didn't move. He stood solid. The screams got louder as Becky's feet thumped down the stairs and then stopped. After a noise like that, the silence rings. Derra moved forward, forcing Cheever against the wall.

'Derra, please, the kids, where are the kids? Please, we are nearly home.'

'Again, Mr Cheever, kids are children, and they are not children anymore. You really don't know anything about us. You have come here with science, but that is no help when things go dry, like here. When life is dry it has edges. Sharp dry edges. A snap, not a chew.' He pressed the knife closer. Cheever exploded into frantic movement and grabbed his wrist with both hands, pushing it up and kicking his knees, and they burst into a messy wrestle before Derra gripped Cheever's chin with his other hand and slammed his forehead onto Cheever's nose. Blood burst out, covering Cheever's face and spattering Derra as he brought the knife back to Cheever's throat and pulled the blade across with a smooth motion. He held Cheever's surprised blood covered crooked nosed face against the wall and considered it before he stepped back and let him slip down until he was the sitting the ground, upright with his back against the wall. Derra ran his hand over his forehead and rubbed it on his apron. He looked down at his hand and at his apron and nodded.

'Messy. Things always get messy. Well a mess from hard work is a good mess. Be proud when you clean it. There is no pride in a lazy mess.'

* * *

In room seventeen, Becky's trembling hands found the keys in Cheever's old brown bag and she sobbed and crawled with as little noise as she could towards the door. The white shapes gathered at the windows, and appeared, ghostly, in the darkness outside. When she got to the door, she could see the swarm of cats spread out as far as the gate. She could hear Froggie. Froggie was curled up in the hull of the old boat trying to stay quiet but his fear pulsed through him, and she could hear his shaking and his broken breathing and his moaning and the sound of his terror spreading across the forecourt.

* * *

Derra sat down cross-legged opposite Cheever who now clutched his swelling face and coughed as his guttural choking pushed blood from his throat. Derra played with the knife, turning it in his hands and looked around. 'I keep this place clean. You see that. I need to. I know why she wants to keep it. I know why she wants to stay here with the cats. To survive. It is the oldest story, Mr Cheever. Survive. When it comes down to it, the choice is taken away. It has to be done. And you know, you scientist, that time changes everything. It will erode, and all that is left of you is the core, what it is you are. What needs to survive. And then you are stuck, you are stuck in that moment. When all there is, is to survive, there is no other moment. Even for you now, bleeding on the floor. Trying to survive. Even for the monster. The old story. There is another word we have. I don't know it in English. Maybe you have something like it. Ampreinyista. It means, um, let me get this right for you, it means a story you know but you don't know. Ignorance of the story that you know. You know the story, you have heard the story, but yet you are ignorant of it. You know how this story goes. You've heard it before. You can even tell it. It's nothing new. But Mr Cheever, it doesn't matter how many times you tell the story, if the story is never understood, then the story is never properly told.'

Cheever slumped sideways onto the floor. The blood had a place to pool. The pot started to boil. Derra stood up and walked to it, leaving red footprints and lifted the lid. He took a large spoon and stirred it, inhaling the scents that rose from the broth, then lowered the flame.

'It will simmer for a while.'

* * *

In the forecourt, the window of the bus reflected the light from the door. It and the old boat had a dull glow, while the sharp blue eyes of the thin white apparitions that were gathered glinted. Becky ran for it. The sound of the bus door slamming and the engine bubbling and shaking made Froggie leap up and fall from the tilt of the small boat and race through the hissing herd of cats who jumped and scraped at him. As the bus caught its engine and Becky turned the big wheel and pressed the accelerator to the floor, he shouted and ran, his heart pumping steel through his core and his eyes wider than ever before, waving his arms furiously until Becky stopped the bus and shouted through tears and terror while he pulled the door open and threw himself inside. Dust rose as the bus sped into the flat dark night. The cats padded back and forth before sliding back into the shadows. The noise of the van disappeared. It was quiet again when Derra's silhouette stopped in the door, dishevelled, still holding the knife. The precious light of the hotel lobby seeped from behind him, but it did not illuminate, it barely touched the desert and the emptiness. It just framed him there.

Lightning Source UK Ltd.
Milton Keynes UK
UKHW010629171020
371753UK00003B/106